REA

ACPL ITEM
ALLEN COUNTY PUBLIC LIBRARY
3 1833 05540 3726

DISCARDED

D0014877

APR 2 4 2009

My Life as a Man

My Life as a Man

FREDERIC LINDSAY

MINOTAUR BOOKS ❧ NEW YORK

This is a work of fiction. All of the characters, organizations, and events portrayed in this novel are either products of the author's imagination or are used fictitiously.

A THOMAS DUNNE BOOK FOR MINOTAUR BOOKS.
An imprint of St. Martin's Publishing Group.

MY LIFE AS A MAN. Copyright © 2006 by Frederic Lindsay. All rights reserved. Printed in the United States of America. For information, address St. Martin's Press, 175 Fifth Avenue, New York, N.Y. 10010.

www.thomasdunnebooks.com
www.minotaurbooks.com

Library of Congress Cataloging-in-Publication Data

Lindsay, Frederic.
    My life as a man / Frederic Lindsay. — 1st U.S. ed.
        p. cm.
    ISBN-13: 978-0-312-37639-0
    ISBN-10: 0-312-37639-1
    1. Scotland—Fiction. I. Title.
    PR6062.I484M9 2009
    823'.914—dc22

                                        2008042970

First published in Great Britain by Polygon, an imprint of Birlinn Ltd

First U.S. Edition: April 2009

10 9 8 7 6 5 4 3 2 1

For Helen

PROLOGUE

Endings

CHAPTER ONE

The day my wife died, 15 February 2003, turned out to be an exceptional day of winter sunshine. It was a day to enjoy the harmless pleasures of self-congratulation: sit in the conservatory, admire the garden and decide we hadn't done too badly with our lives. We'd been married a long time. That morning, though, Eileen had a different idea.

'I want you to go on the demonstration,' she said.

I knew at once what she was talking about. The previous day's papers had been full of them, demonstrations all over the world, and today Glasgow was having its very own.

'What's it got to do with us?' I wondered. 'Let them all get on with it.'

'I'd go myself,' she said, 'if I was able.'

She was in bed, on her lap the breakfast tray I'd brought up to her. We'd spent the previous afternoon in the park at Rouken Glen. We'd walked hand in hand, though normally she didn't like holding hands in public. Maybe we'd walked too far, but the weather had been fine that day, too. Today she was tired.

'It's not the kind of thing we do,' I said. 'What do we care about politics?'

'It's time we cared. When you think there are boys now giving the Nazi salute – even in Russia! – it breaks my heart. Have they no memory?' She stared at me. 'What is there to smile at in that?'

'Something just came into my head. Tony, my best friend at school, his wee brother ate a banana with its skin on. Just after the war. He'd never seen one before. The things you remember, eh?'

'You're a silly man,' she said.

'But I made you smile. I don't want you brooding on ancient

history and stuff like that.' Concentration camps again in Europe. Skeletons behind barbed wire again. Maybe even butchers with tears in their eyes listening to Brahms. 'Not on a day like this. We could walk round the garden with a glass of wine after lunch.'

'Oh, the garden,' she said sardonically.

I smiled at her. 'We're a nation of two.'

'Like Switzerland?'

'There are worse countries to be.'

Her hair was white and she had wrinkles on her face, but sometimes when I looked at her I didn't just see her as a young woman, I saw the girl she must have been long before we met. She had surprised me and I was moved and impressed. She was almost ninety, but her heart was younger than mine for she still cared about the world.

'Do you ever think of August and Beate?' she asked.

I was startled. In all these years, we had never spoken of them.

'Hardly ever,' I said.

It wasn't a lie, though for a long time it would have been.

'That night we ran away from them, I shouldn't have stopped you from seeing,' she said.

'Whatever it was they were doing, God help them, we could probably watch worse now on television,' I said. 'Nothing's censored now.' I wanted to make her smile, change the subject, anything but this talk of the past.

'I know you've thought about it,' she said.

'Not for a long time.'

'It would have been better to see what happened that night. Maybe if you had, that would have been the end of it. You'd have thought less about it if you'd seen.'

That she could make me feel guilty was ridiculous. I wasn't a child caught masturbating, the pink balloon of an adult's face above bedclothes thrown back.

Managing a smile, I asked, 'Is that why I am to go and demonstrate?'

'Please,' she said quietly. She knew I was angry. I couldn't hide anything from her.

'If it means that much to you, I'll go,' I said. 'Even if I have to go alone.'

'I'll be with you in spirit,' she said.

The sunshine was bad luck for Tony Blair, the prime minister. By the time I got to Glasgow Green, where the peace march was scheduled to start, a great crowd was already assembling. Some people like crowds. I'm not fond of them, not even on the pavements of Argyle Street or Sauchiehall Street in the middle of a Saturday afternoon, though I'd kept Eileen company in the days when she enjoyed the bustle.

It was a good-natured crowd. Sunshine does that. It makes you feel good, brightening the colours of women's coats, burnishing the stone of the old buildings, warm on your cheek or the back of your neck. Feeling good about themselves, too, that makes people happy; all of them sure that they were doing the right thing, which as it happened I didn't feel certain about at all.

'Coming along was my wife's idea,' I told Tom and Margaret, a couple I'd just met. The three of us had exchanged names in a kind of holiday mood. 'She feels strongly that going to war is wrong.'

They both spoke at once.

He asked, 'So how do you feel about it?'

She asked, 'Your wife isn't here? I hope she's not ill?'

To her, I said, 'Oh, no, no. She keeps good health, but the walk would be too much for her.'

She gave me a shrewd look. At a guess, she and her husband and I were all about the same age, somewhere in the late sixties. All presumably, as I'd claimed for my wife, in good health; all able to walk the few miles from the rallying point to the Scottish Exhibition and Conference Centre, outside which the demonstration would be held, while inside the Scottish Labour Party was holding its spring conference.

Now the crowd was drifting steadily forward. We filled two paths and the police were letting people through to join the procession first from one path, then the other. When they let us through, I looked at my watch and it was quarter past eleven.

Walking along in the sunshine, I felt caught up in something bigger than myself. It was strange to feel safe in the middle of such a crowd. On the way, Tom – for the three of us had stayed together – suggested that we should turn aside to buy something to eat. It was foolish but none of us had thought of what to do for our lunch. Margaret spotted a café and we went in and bought filled rolls and I bought lemonade; they had brought a bottle of water with them, though they hadn't any food.

By the time we got to the gates of the Centre, it was just before two o'clock. We found a place on a grass bank above the car park. The crowd had been gathered into two of the car parks in front of the Centre; there were plenty of other parks for cars. I looked from the building ahead, its roofs folded one on top of the other like the scales on an armadillo, to the tower behind us that led down into the walkway under the Clyde. We shared the last of the rolls – cheese and pickle, coronation chicken, ham and tomato – and sipped lemonade out of the bottle.

'Look,' Tom said, 'they've got sound equipment after all.'

I said it was what I'd have expected, two big speakers, set up one on either side of the platform.

'Thing is,' Margaret said, 'Labour refused to let them use a PA system.'

'How could they do that? What has the Labour Party to do with the car parks?'

'The council owns the SECC,' Tom said.

He waited till the penny dropped, and then grinned. The Labour Party has run Glasgow for ever, it seems.

'Well, they must have changed their mind,' I said. 'You can see the speakers.'

'Or had it changed for them,' Margaret said. 'There was a demonstration a week ago, and they were told that not to have a PA system wouldn't be safe.'

'We got a leaflet about it,' Tom said, 'from CND a week ago.'

'CND?' I said.

'Ageing hippies, that's us,' Tom said. 'I know.'

Across the murmur of the crowd, the sound system carried the voice of a man who'd been introduced as a councillor. 'I've just

6

been told the police estimate there are twenty-seven thousand people here. Well, all I can say is, the Glasgow police cannae count!'

'Right enough,' Tom said. 'Comparing this with the big football crowds they used to get, I'd say there was three times that. Maybe more.'

After that we listened for a while to the voices booming from the little figures on the platform. John Swinney, leader of the SNP, talked about the need for a UN resolution; a man from the TUC spoke, and then the leader of the Fire Brigades Union. Like the preacher and sin, all of them it seemed were against going to war in Iraq. After about an hour, the voices got fainter, as if the address system was using batteries and they were running down. By the time it got to Tommy Sheridan, the Socialist leader, you couldn't make out what he was saying, though even at a distance you could tell he cared, which made me envy him. Nice to feel that anything mattered that much.

By this time, it was about three o'clock and Margaret said her back was sore with standing. There didn't seem anything to stay for, though as we left people were still streaming into the car parks. It was good to be strolling along on a fine afternoon, it still felt like being part of a crowd. Somewhere up ahead there was a guy with a trombone and every so often he gave us a tune.

'Pity about the Jericho Rumpus,' Tom said.

'Is that what he's playing?'

'What?'

'The guy with the trombone.'

Tom smiled reluctantly. It was Margaret who realised I wasn't trying to be funny. Truth is, I'm tone-deaf; I was willing to believe anything.

'Everybody was supposed to bring something to make a noise,' she said. 'Pans, drums, whatever. The rumpus would start up about half past one and the idea was that Blair would hear it inside the hall while he was speaking.'

'Except that he changed the time. They got his speech before they'd digested their ham and eggs, and by eleven in the morning he was on his way back to London.'

7

By the time we'd walked all the way into Argyle Street it was after four o'clock. With all that fresh air, they were hungry and decided to go into the café in Woolworth's for something to eat before they caught the bus home to East Kilbride. I don't know why I went with them. I was hungry, of course, from the fresh air, but I wasn't all that far from home. Truth is, I'd enjoyed the excitement of the day, the bustle. We led a quiet life, Eileen and I.

They got fish and chips and a pot of tea. I was tempted but I stuck to coffee and a piece of cake.

When we were settled at a table, Tom said, 'You know what I was thinking as we were coming back along the road there?' He shook his head. 'I was thinking, we never learn. From Aldermaston on, doesn't matter how big the crowd is, the government does what it wants.'

'That's no excuse for not trying,' Margaret said.

'Maybe it's time to hang up our boots,' Tom said. 'Leave it to the younger folk.'

'Anything for an argument. You know fine it'll always be worth trying for the children's sake,' his wife said. I realised from the sharing quality of her smile that she assumed I had children, too. I didn't correct her.

'Maybe human beings are too stupid to worry about.'

'That's a terrible thing to say!'

'And there's no sauce,' Tom said. He got up and went back to the counter.

'He's a worrier,' Margaret said. 'If it wasn't this, it would be global warming. Sitting brooding's no good for you. You have to get out and do something. Isn't that right?'

'To be honest with you, this is the first time I've ever been on any kind of march,' I told her. 'I'm not what you'd call a political animal. I wouldn't be here if it wasn't for my wife.'

'It's often the way. It's natural for a woman to care more than a man.'

I wasn't sure how true that was, but didn't feel strongly enough to argue about it.

Tom came back with a bottle of tomato sauce. He banged the

bottom of it a couple of times to put some on the edge of his plate.

'Harry says he's never been on a demonstration before,' his wife told him.

'It's amazing how many people are the same,' he said. 'First-timers like you. I've been puzzling my head to think why. Why do people care so much about whether or not we go to war with Iraq? I'm not talking about the usual suspects like Margaret and me.' Abstractedly, he took his wife by the hand, a public gesture of affection which seemed to startle her. 'Or the ones who'd turn out for anything as long as it was anti-American. But we're being told there are a million people on the streets down in London and millions more in France and Germany and Italy and all over the world. Why is that? Do you know what I think? It's the millennium.'

'It can't just be that going to war is wrong?' his wife said.

'That, of course,' he said with a touch of impatience. 'But the sheer *scale* of all that's been happening.' He shook his head again. 'No, I think people wanted things to be different with the end of the Cold War. We'd all been frightened for so long: waiting for the end of the world. And then the Berlin Wall came down and just for a year or two everything looked better. I think all of this' – he waved a hand as if the crowded pavements outside were part of the same great demonstration – 'is pure disappointment. It's saying, I know we can't stop the madness, but we can tell history we didn't like where we were going. It's one way of saying sorry to the future.'

'To the children,' his wife said.

Their sincerity made me uncomfortable. 'Time for me to be getting off home,' I said. 'The wife'll be wanting to know how it all went.'

'Tell her it was worth it,' Margaret said.

It wasn't often now that I travelled on a bus, and so I enjoyed sitting on the top deck on the way home. I watched the tenements fall behind and saw the tall blocks of the high-rises in the distance, and remembered my boyhood in a room and kitchen and later in one of the houses in the schemes they'd built after the war to decant the poor out of their poverty; the excitement of having an inside lavatory and a bathroom and a garden at the back. And now I was going home to a house, bought after we got up the courage to come back to Glasgow, with a wall at the side that enclosed a garage and a yard behind it and a hedge and a lawn and another hedge and a garden of roses right at the end. We'd lived there ever since, happily, oh, ideally happily, though we had acquired from that terrible time with August and Beate a habit of holding our breath and we continued to hold it even when there was no need, as if only by keeping still would we be safe. And so all the causes and the politics and what people marched and demonstrated about had passed us by, and it only occurred to me as late as this that it might have been for my sake, not hers.

Quarter of an hour later I was stretched on the floor beside her. She must have got up to tidy the tray away. A plate and a broken cup were by the wall where they had been thrown from her as she fell. All day she must have been alone there while the crowds were gathering, while the speeches were being made, while I walked in the sun. I clasped her hand with its poor bent fingers and waited as if she might open her eyes, though I knew she never would or ever could again. The curtain was drawn still against the morning and in that shadowy light all the days I had lived became one as I lay bereft.

BOOK ONE

Father and Son

CHAPTER TWO

When I was a child, my father, Tommy Glass, drove things for a living. A long-distance lorry driver for a while, he gave that up so he could be home more. It's funny the way things work out. He got a job on the docks, and when the war came that meant he was in a reserved occupation. This night I'm thinking of, he came home with an armful of books. As he set them down on the kitchen table, he must have asked where my mother was. Stupid question: she didn't share her plans with me any more than she did with him. I'm talking now of years ago and so I can't remember exactly how I pointed that out – 'I don't know where she is,' said with a scowl, I'd guess; not knowing yet how lucky I was to have him there – but I remember his answer. 'Who's "she"?' he asked. Not that he didn't know, but he thought it was disrespectful of me at eleven to say 'she' instead of 'Mummy'.

He liked to cook, so there was one way I was lucky with him. He didn't have a big range: fish and chips, toasted cheese with a poached egg on top, scrambled eggs, mince and tatties. As for what he made that night, that's gone; not that it could possibly matter, though I've tried to remember. Probably not the mince and tatties: cooked up in a pot with turnip and carrots, that took time, and his detour up Maryhill Road to the library had made him late. Whatever it was, it would have been good; everything he made tasted good. But I shoved my plate away, maybe took a mouthful or two, maybe stirred my fork round in it, for sure shoved the plate away. I remember the way he looked at me when I did that. I should have been hungry. I'd been alone in the house since four o'clock. Chances are there would have been bread and jam; probably I'd stuffed myself on bread and jam.

He ate one-handed while he read. I stayed at the table even though I wasn't eating. When I caught him glancing up at me, he nodded at the pile of books and said, 'Anything there you fancy?'

And he meant anything, though every one of them was out of the adult library. I could look through whatever was there, no rhyme or reason to what he chose, not that I could see, all kinds of books caught his eye. Often, impatient, he'd pick up and lay down book after book, so that all of them went back unfinished. I used to wonder what he could be searching for that was so hard to find.

'No,' I said.

'You haven't looked.'

'I don't need to. It'll be rubbish.'

'Where have I heard that before?' It was a word my mother used a lot. Shaking his head, he went on before I could open my mouth. 'Found another one about King Arthur.'

'We've finished with him.'

'So what's your teacher got you on now? I'll look next time I'm in the library.'

'Nothing.' Why was I angry? Maybe I was tired of coming into an empty house.

He pulled out a book from the pile and turned it so I could see the cover.

'I was on my way out when I spotted it on the returns shelf. Don't know what it's like, but they're all in there, Arthur, Gawain, Lancelot, sitting around in their tin underwear waiting for a knock at the door to go off on an adventure.' He pushed it over to me. 'Have a look, Harry.'

I pushed it back without a glance and got up to put on the wireless, too loud, I expect; that was a bad habit of mine. I'm pretty sure he sat on, reading at the table. What I remember is waking up during the night with the noise of the outside door slamming shut. Lying in the dark in the recess bed in the kitchen, I heard my father's voice in the lobby and then my mother answering him. The voices weren't angry or loud, and listening to them I fell asleep again. As usual, by the time I was up in the morning he'd gone to work.

When I got back from school, I looked in the bedroom, half

expecting to see my mother hitched up on the pillow with a cup of tea, and a fag in her mouth, but there was only a tangle of blankets on the empty bed. In the kitchen, I made myself a piece and jam, took my father's seat at the table and picked up the book he'd left there for me. Because of the crown on his head, you could tell which one was supposed to be Arthur in the picture on the cover. He looked older than the others, and as if he had a lot on his mind. Lancelot was easy, too, long blond hair surrounded by light as if someone had left a door open to the sun. The book was too old for me, not a book of stories at all. Like a penance, I persisted with it, until I was left with a handful of words: medieval, chivalry, and in a footnote *The Romance of the Rose*. The main thing was that I'd looked at it. I wanted to be able to tell my father when he came home that I'd looked at it; but he didn't come home, not that night or any other. Later we heard that he'd given up working on the docks, and then that he'd been called up. For a while, every time I walked past Maryhill Barracks I wondered if he was somewhere on the other side of the high wall with its ugly shards of broken glass.

My mother said he must have been planning to leave. 'He wouldn't have the guts to say anything to me about meeting another woman. I should never have agreed to marry him. When I told him I was pregnant, "Marry me, Nettie," he said, and like a fool I did.'

She went on like that for years afterwards, whenever she thought of it. I learned not to argue about it, but no one else ever said anything about him being with another woman, and if he'd been planning to leave us what kind of sense did it make that he'd brought home all those books that night, and among them one for me? Why would he have done that?

BOOK TWO

The Age of Chivalry

CHAPTER THREE

Monday morning the new job made a reason to get up. I almost didn't, though, which as things turned out would have been a pity. Most mornings I lay until the bang of the front door signalled I would have the house to myself. That would be somewhere around half eight and I'd get up and scrounge for breakfast, bread and something to put on it, a cup of tea.

When I went barefoot into the kitchen, he was in his underpants at the sink filling the kettle. His name was Alec Turner, though I thought of him as the Hairy Bastard, and we'd shared the house since my mother walked out on him a year earlier, when I was seventeen.

'What happened to you? You fall out of bed?'

'You might have given me a shout,' I complained. 'I'm starting work this morning.'

He gave me a look that would have soured milk and went out without saying anything. I was on my second cup of tea when he came back, opened the cupboard under the sink and started to scratch around in the rubbish pail.

'What do you call that?' Down on his hunkers, holding it up at the stretch of his arm to stick it under my nose.

'What would you call it?' I asked.

'I'd call it empty. That was for my supper last night.'

'Oh, aye.' There didn't seem anything to say to that. I put the kettle on the ring and lit the gas.

'You listening to me, Harry?' He smelled of bed sweat and sweet aftershave in the morning. It was a smell I'd hated since at fourteen I'd seen him for the first time and realised my mother must have brought him back with her from the dancing the night before.

'Are you listening to me, you wee shit?'

When I turned round, I was looking down on his bald patch. Hair everywhere else, not only on his chest, but a pelt of it on his back and little tufts on the back of his fingers. Plus smell. Not that he wasn't clean enough; no aroma of piss, nothing like that. Jungly smell. Maybe it went with being such a hairy bastard. Me Tarzan, you Nettie.

'I want you out of here, boy.'

'Where am I supposed to go?'

'You should have thought of that.'

'Before I ate your bloody corned beef?' That came out wrong, with a wee touch of panic, not tough at all. He'd given me crap before about throwing me out, but this time was different. It's odd how I knew that right away.

He'd been palming a key for the front door and now he slid it into sight with his thumb, tricky as a conjuror. Mine had been on top of my jacket on a chair beside the bed, ready to pick up on my way out. When I went to check, it wasn't there. And he'd dumped everything out of the drawers all over the bed.

'You've ten minutes to pack,' he said, following me in.

When I'd finished, I looked at the shelf of books. You can't carry a shelf of books on your back. One, though? Maybe two? There were some it would hurt me to leave. And what about the library books? Something to remember me by. Getting postcards about fines would drive him crazy.

'What's the fucking joke?' he asked. 'Your head's never out of a book or stuck up your arse. You're useless. From now on, boy, you're in the real world and I'll tell you what chance you've got. No chance, you've got no chance.'

'I'll tell you one thing I've got, I've got a job,' I said. He didn't break into applause, just sneered and shook his head. 'Mr Simpson put me on to it, the one that did careers when I was at North Kelvinside. I met him in the street, and he asked me what I was doing.' You could have made more of yourself, he'd told me.

'Schoolteacher arsehole.' He had a gift for that kind of repartee.

'He was all right.'

'You wee poof!' he said and pointed at the wall without waiting for an answer. 'That goes with you, by the way!'

I never had gone in for posters, so the only thing on the wall was a picture I'd torn out of a magazine. Don't ask me why I'd put it there with a strip of Scotch tape top and bottom. Not because of his long blond hair, that was for sure, or because, Christ, I fancied him. A picture of a knight on horseback. Why not? There were worse things you could stick on a wall.

'I won't get paid till Friday. If you want me to leave, I'll leave then.'

'Today – I've a friend coming.'

'Who?' He didn't have any friends as far as I knew, just people he drank with until sooner or later they got sick of one another. A nasty thought struck me. 'You talking about a woman?'

'That's my business.' But he couldn't stop himself from giving a wee smirk.

'You tell her about Nettie?'

He sneered at me. 'Nettie, is it? You mean your mammy?'

'Did you?'

'What would I do that for? Your fucking head's wasted.'

'Is whoever-she-is moving in?'

'Before she steps in that door, I want you on the other side of it. And that's it. Out, finished, on your own. No more charity.'

'I've more right here than you have. If my mother was here, she wouldn't let you get away with it. You only walked in here five minutes ago.' Wrong on all counts, as a matter of fact. In reverse order: he'd been here for years, and who could ever tell what Nettie would do? Third, and the one that mattered, my bloody mother had signed papers that made him the tenant. Love's young dream.

'I'm a fool to myself,' he said. 'I've been good to you.'

On the other side of the road I put the rucksack down. I'd pocketed the spare key on my way out; God knows why; a souvenir of good times? I took a last look: end of a terrace of pebble-dashers, a cold box with four rooms. Built after the war, lines and miles of them dumped on the edges of the city, no pubs, no pictures, crap wee shops. Metal frames showed in straps along the edges of the wall in every room, like the skeleton on an insect. The competition to get one of them was terrific. Everyone wanted out of the old tenements, so there was a points system. Points for how long you'd been on the waiting list and points for how many children you had. My mother just had me, but the two of us got a house. Rumour had it that she'd slept with a councillor. That's the kind of rumour somebody always wants to share with you. Since then, the garden had gone to hell in long tangles of sick-looking grass, a colour of its own as if the earth had taken a scunner at us. Under the window of my bedroom upstairs the pebble-dash had flaked off like patches of acne. Funny thing is, that hadn't happened to any of the other houses. We were always an embarrassment to the neighbours.

Home. That was one way of describing a place I'd never liked, but walking down the road I couldn't think of another one.

CHAPTER FOUR

By bus the factory was ten minutes away. The plan had been to walk it, but with all the nonsense I didn't have time. After paying the fare, I had a handful of silver between me and pay day on Friday. Getting off the bus, I wasn't looking for much, just a proper job where you got up in the morning, went home after a shift, got paid at the end of the week. I didn't know where I was going to sleep that night. If somebody had told me, see this job you've got, you're going to be working there for the next thirty years, I'd have said bloody wonderful.

The way it turned out, I lasted five days.

That very first morning I saw her sitting in the car, but I was too busy worrying about being late to pay attention. I'd got off the bus on a side road with shitty wasteland behind me and in front a building behind a high link metal fence. I walked along by the fence, looking for a way in, and started to panic when I couldn't find one. When I got to the corner, the fence stretched away along the side street but I still couldn't see any sign of a gate. I started down that street, changed my mind and hurried all the way back to where I'd started. Through the link fence, the place seemed empty of life. Even when I went round the far corner and found there was a gate, I couldn't see anyone. Where were they all? How late was I? Had I got the start time wrong? Why couldn't I see anyone going into work? It was like one of those nightmares that don't make any sense, and all the time the clock was ticking. Inside, I half ran into the first opening and found myself in a little courtyard with a car parked by the wall. I didn't know much about cars, but it was a big one – you didn't need to be an expert to see that – and it had been polished until it shone. The windows were steamed up.

In the wing mirror, I could see my hair standing on end and

the sweat on my face. Don't ask me what I thought I was doing when I went to the window. Looking for directions? Bending down, I got so close that I could see a girl's face turned to look at me. Not clearly – she didn't wipe the glass or roll down the window – and I stared in until it occurred to me I might be frightening her.

Straightening up, I saw a door in the wall with the firm's name on a sign so discreet it was no wonder I hadn't noticed it.

As I went in, a racket like machine-gun fire stopped abruptly. Behind a long counter, a woman was sitting with her back to me. Alerted by something, maybe a colder movement of the air, she whipped her head round from the typewriter and stared at me. 'Staff don't come in this door,' she said. I hadn't even opened my mouth. It was as if she knew at first glance I was a mistake; but then I suppose that's what she was paid for.

Turning, I saw a door at the back marked STAFF ONLY.

'Not that way. Go back outside,' she said, 'through the swing doors. You're not supposed to go in from here.'

'Sounds like a joke.' She looked down her nose at me, and I made the mistake of trying to explain. It was a joke my father had been fond of, an old joke. 'You know, "If you want to go to Dublin you shouldn't start from here."'

A man in shirtsleeves came round a partition at the back and stared at me.

Like the Kerry man trying to get to Dublin, it wasn't a good start.

CHAPTER FIVE

The second morning, seeing the same car in the same place and steam on the windows was a surprise. Determined not to be late, I was early, so I'd gone round that way to kill time, never imagining she'd be there again. Not that I could be sure she was, since I didn't dare go into the yard for a closer look. But, if not her, someone was in the car or why else would the windows be steamed up?

'She's there all day,' one of the women on the line said.

'The girl,' the other one said and laughed.

I'd asked, first chance I got, 'Who's the girl in the car?'

'What car would that be?'

'Dozens of cars out there.'

Comedians.

'I'm talking about the wee park round the side. Not the big one at the front.'

'What about it?'

'There's a girl sits in a car there in the morning.'

'All day,' she said then. 'The girl,' the other one said. You could tell they thought they were funny. They laughed at their own jokes. They stood on either side of a press, and my job for that part of the day was to take away the full bin of castings and slot in an empty one. Hearing them wasn't easy. The big space echoed with the fart and whine of machines that dribbled oil to make rainbows on the pools of scummy water under where the corrugated-iron roof leaked.

'All day, every day.'

'Until *he* leaves.'

'Who?' I wanted to know.

They ignored me, talking to each other.

'He's away before us.'

'Put it that way.'

'That'll be why you might think she was just there in the morning.'

'Instead of the whole bloody day.'

'Morning till night.'

'Right enough, you can't see, not from here.'

'But he can. Out of his window, he can see. He can see, all right.'

All through this, they never stopped working. Their hands made the same movements over and over again. Hands and tongues, they never stopped.

'Catch me putting up with it.'

'Catch you getting the chance.'

'Maybe it's worth it.'

'More ways than one, maybe.' She had a dirty laugh.

'Not for money, not for the other, not in a million years. It gives me the creeps.'

'He likes to keep an eye on her.'

The one who said that laughed again, but this time her face didn't laugh.

Something about the joke wasn't funny. All day I couldn't stop thinking about it.

What kind of man made a girl sit outside all day? And the question that really bothered me: a girl who would do that, what kind of girl would she be? I was so distracted, I went the wrong way when the foreman switched jobs on me, and pushed the bin through two sets of doors without giving it a thought. It was the brightness that stopped me in my tracks. The sound of the machinery in here was different, and everything was clean and new-looking. I hardly had time to take in the size of the place, when I was punched on the shoulder.

'What are you playing at?'

I followed the foreman along the corridor between the doors. Without looking round, he said, 'Keep out of there.'

'Is that a different firm?'

'Don't be stupid,' he said.

'What are they making?'

'A special truncheon that works as a whip one way and club the other – that one's export only.' He grinned. 'It's used on Death Row in the States.'

'What?'

'Forget it, I'm joking,' and marching off he let the doors swing back on me as I followed.

The women weren't much more helpful.

'They make all kinds of different stuff,' one of them assured me.

'And the money's good. See, if you get through there? You're on a different rate.'

'I don't like it,' I said.

'Don't bother your head about it, son. A job's a job. You need a job, there's plenty worse than this one. Anyways, most of it goes abroad. It's no for here.'

'Who cares where it's for?' the other one said, frowning. It was the first time I'd seen parts slipping past her on the belt, like a stutter, her quick hands missing a beat.

That night I dreamed I was riding across a bridge, in armour. In the water I saw myself mirrored, metal gloves on my hands, a plume of feathers on my helmet. I was going to rescue the girl in the castle and if I had to kill to do it, that was all right. I had a sword.

My first thought on Wednesday morning was for the girl. I was as tired as if I hadn't slept, but I went the long way round the building to check if her car was there.

Seeing it, I couldn't bring myself to walk on. After a minute looking, I took a step towards it, then another. Just then, a face round and white as a plate appeared at the first-floor window. That was all it took to spin me round and set me scurrying off with cockcrow in my ears.

I went into the factory with my mind made up. I'd keep on asking until I found out all there was to know about her. But when I came out of the lavatory (the smell of piss up my nose, if you sat on the toilet holes poked in the partitions at eye height, brown stains in the wash basin . . . thirty years of this; did I say thirty years?) I found the foreman, Ronnie, going through my

27

rucksack, and that put it out of my head. I'd been leaving the rucksack under a bench where the coats were hung, and there he was down on his knees with the straps undone and the flap thrown back.

'You're sleeping rough,' he said. He pulled out a shirt, and the pair of underpants wound in it fell out on the floor. 'What kind of day's work you going to do if you're sleeping rough?'

CHAPTER SIX

Thursday night it went wrong. Since the Hairy Bastard threw me out, I'd been sleeping on Tony's bedroom floor. There are people like that, nice guys you think of first when you need a favour. All he asked was that I was out of there before his parents got up. At least it meant for three days I got to work early enough to check the car in the private car park.

Thursday night I was outside their flat at half eleven on the dot, which was our arrangement, waiting for Tony to open the door and slip me inside. Time passed. I'd walked around for hours; I was starving. I could hardly wait to get inside. Tony would have made sandwiches, the way he'd done the other nights – he was a decent guy. I put my ear to the door, then got down on my hunkers and lifted the flap of the letterbox. There were coats hung behind the door, but I could hear screaming and shouting.

When the door opened, it nearly pulled me off my feet. I tried to push it further open and Tony's voice whispered, 'May's home.'

'So what?'

'She's up the stick.' A good job in London, I'd heard his father boasting, not just a pretty face. Now big sister was home and looking for somebody to hold the baby. A bit old-fashioned, but it was a family tragedy, I'm not stupid, I could see that.

'I only need one more night,' I said.

'No chance, Harry. None of us'll—' His head whipped round as if somebody had come into the lobby behind him. 'The old man's going mental. None of us'll get any sleep tonight,' he said, and nearly took my nose off, he shut the door so fast.

That night I slept rough.

I didn't have the hang of it. I hadn't even the sense to put another shirt out of the rucksack on top of the one I was wearing. When I woke up in the morning at the back of a close, my legs had gone numb and my neck felt as if I'd grown a hump overnight. I thought it must be time to go to work, but there were hours still to go. I walked about, and the rain came on just after it got light. No bread, no cheese, no slug of milk out of Tony's kitchen before his folk were up. Pissing against a wall in a backcourt. A woman shot up her window and yelled down at me. The hygiene Gestapo. There was a guy in a long black coat used to beg in Kelvingrove Park when the good weather arrived, ambushed the girls in particular, held out his hand, never said a word, challenged them with a stare. I mean, this was a fierce-looking guy, except that every spring he'd shrunk a little and one came when he wasn't around any more. Winters are cold this far north.

I bought breakfast at a corner shop. A macaroon bar wiped me out. Not a penny left. Well, one. I threw it up and toed it into the road. Thank God it was Friday.

Strange thing is, seeing the car with its windows steamed up that morning, I envied her, sitting inside in comfort, warm and out of the rain.

Funny, too, how quickly I'd fallen into the routine of the work. It wasn't hard and, for sure, didn't take any brains. One of the other boys, a long drink of water called Sammy, grumbled at me, 'What you whistling for? I'm bored out of my skull. This place is shite.' Sammy the intellectual; but as for me, sad case that I was, the truth is I was enjoying myself. Boring was lying in bed because you couldn't face getting up. No, the smell of oil, the heat, the clatter of metal, the fact everybody was busy or pretending to be was fine by me. I liked all of it.

I even liked being curious about the three men who appeared in the middle of the morning. Two were tall, one with a long, narrow face and gold-framed glasses, the other built like a farmer with a red-brown slab of a face and heavy jowls; the third man was different, just under middle height, and he swaggered like a weightlifter whose thighs were too big for easy walking. The man I'd seen at the office on my first day was escorting them. He'd been in shirtsleeves then. Now he had his jacket on, and was waving his hands and talking nineteen to the dozen. I suppose they were listening to him, though the elegant man seemed to pay no attention, glancing from side to side through his gold-framed glasses as the four of them went down the line of machines. They walked the length of the place quickly; important men with no time to waste, and vanished through the door into the other unit.

I thought it was interesting. I didn't mind the way the elegant man had looked at us.

'Like dirt under his feet,' one of the women said. Hands never still as tongues wagged. 'Specky bastard.'

Middle of the afternoon, the foreman, Ronnie, came round with the pay slips. Rule was they weren't supposed to be checked until the break, but right away the grumbling started about deductions, how the overtime was shared, aches and pains from the repetitive work, and from there somehow to the refrain about how useless men were in general and in particular here in the factory and most particularly the ones they were saddled with at home.

When I went after him, Ronnie said, 'Nothing for you.' He had one of those old wanker moustaches like a bandit in a Gene Autry movie. *Down Mexico Way.* 'Lying time. A week's lying time. Don't give me crap you weren't told.'

Liars' time.

'You mean I worked this week for nothing?'

Swindlers' time.

'You get it when you leave the job.'

Bastards' time.

'I need it now.'

'Tough. You should have listened when you were tellt.'

I didn't even take time to think. I went out the usual exit, marched all the way round the building and in the front door. It was raining again. The receptionist was in the same place, not typing or answering a phone this time, just staring out at the rain. She curled her lip at me; maybe it was the only thing she'd moved since Monday.

'Can I speak to the boss?'

'You want to see Mr Bernard?'

How ridiculous! But part of the comedy was a glance at the stairs when she said his name. I took the hint and headed for them, her voice shrilling behind me as I took the blue-carpeted steps two at a time.

There was a landing with three doors. Through the open one I saw a fat man down on his knees, resting his belly on the bottom drawer of a filing cabinet.

'Mr Bernard?'

'Eh?'

'It's about my lying time.'

'What's that to do with me?' He lost his balance and tipped slowly forward, pushing the drawer shut with his belly.

'I can't wait a week for my money.'

'Why not?' a voice asked behind me. He was in shirtsleeves, like the first time I'd seen him. 'I'm Mr Bernard,' he said.

I stood in front of his desk and couldn't stop talking. That hadn't been the idea, but he was a good listener. He sat there turning a pen in his fingers and nodding. No hurry; it was as if he had all the time in the world. Who was this exactly who'd thrown me out? How long had my mother been gone? This Tony, he was such a good friend, why'd I have to leave? His sister was pregnant? When he grinned, I smiled back without getting the joke.

That was the other thing. I wanted him to like me. I don't mean because he was the boss or because I needed my money; I'd have wanted him to like me anyway. I don't need to be told how stupid that sounds, but I think most people would have felt the same way – I mean if they'd met him in a pub or at a wedding or a party somewhere. He had a tan, not the kind you got frying on a holiday beach, but as if he was out of doors a lot of the time, and you could imagine him playing tennis or golf or skiing, all that kind of stuff. He wasn't as tall as I was, but he was broad built. A man who could take care of himself, but not one who'd go looking for trouble; more as if he'd rather swap stories – and his would be good, you'd want to hear what happened to him. A man with a sense of humour.

Listening, he smiled a couple of times and never took his eyes off my face as if he was really interested in what I had to say. I'd hesitate and he'd nod, go on, and I did. I told him my life story.

He must have signalled for her because the receptionist came in without knocking. He said, 'This is Mr Gas.'

'Glass,' I said.

'He went right past me.' She scowled at me, but at the same time she shifted her weight. It was as if she didn't know she was doing it, but one hip swung towards him and the dress tightened across her belly.

'Talk to you about that later.' He lifted a case from under the desk and handed it to her with a bunch of keys he took from his pocket. 'Put this in the boot. Oh, and Theresa, I want you to arrange for the young chap here to be paid a week's wages. Here's the authorisation.'

He scribbled on a pad, tore the note off and gave it to her. Looking back, it embarrasses me how much I thanked him. I was following her out, when he said, 'Mr Gas.'

'Yes, sir?' I was thinking, What does it matter if he gets my name wrong? I'll get it right with the girl when they pay me.

'This man your mother left.'

I was taken aback by that. I glanced at the receptionist, but she was reading the note he'd given her.

'Sir?'

Where I was standing, I could see down into a little private car park. I realised this must be the window I'd seen the man looking down from, looking down at me beside the car, the car with the girl in it. The car was still there, the windows still steamed up.

'The hairy gentleman. He ever get into bed with you?'

He snorted laughter and gave a big smile and I smiled back. What else was I supposed to do?

'Good-looking boy like you,' he said.

When the receptionist and I passed the open door, the fat man was still kneeling beside the cabinet. He looked a little desperate and there were files piled knee high around him on the floor. His face had gone bright red, and as we passed he cried out, 'You could have told the boy to speak to me.' His voice was thin and pitched very high. It was unexpected coming from someone that size.

'Sorry,' the receptionist drawled, not sounding sorry at all.

'I could have dealt with it. I'm saying I can deal with a staff problem just as well as Bernard.'

Who was he? Somebody who kept the books? Not that it mattered. A fat man.

'It's been attended to,' she said, giving a little shake in his direction of the note Mr Bernard had given her.

'Let me see.' He struggled up and took it from her. After a moment, he sighed and gave it back.

'Do you have a bank account?' she asked me. 'It says to pay you by cheque.'

I stared at her; there was no answer to that.

He blew out his breath, 'Oh, for Christ's sake! Give him his money in cash.' In disgust he pulled out more files. He wasn't looking at either of us and I saw his sweat shine in the fluorescent light. 'Just do it,' he said. 'Please.'

I went back determined to show how hard I could work. For Mr Bernard. I was going to be a fan. First, though, I needed a pee. Even the toilets didn't seem so manky. I used one of the stalls and checked the money. It wasn't as much as I'd hoped – I'd forgotten about deductions – but that was all right. Then I read the bit at the bottom.

Lying time.

You got it when you were finished. First week, last week. I was finished.

This time I went through the factory, along a corridor and through the door for STAFF ONLY to where the receptionist was just coming back in from the outside. The telephone on her desk was ringing and I followed her round the counter, crowding at her heels.

As she turned, startled, 'You've made a mistake,' I told her and held out the pay slip.

'No, I haven't.' She picked up the telephone, but covered the mouthpiece for a moment with her hand. 'I did what I was told to do.' She had an unfortunate manner, but she probably wasn't a bad person.

When she began to talk into the phone, she turned away and spoke too quietly for me to hear. It's possible she was embarrassed for me, this poor bastard, given the bullet, no thirty years, no gold watch. Career over before it started.

What had the women on the production line said? 'But he can. Out of his window, he can see. He can see, all right.' Now I knew who 'he' was.

She'd laid the bunch of keys on her desk and I picked them up. All the way out I expected to hear her yelling after me.

I opened the door of the car and said, 'Mrs Bernard?'

'Mrs Morton,' she said.

I got in and switched on. The engine was beautiful. You could hardly hear it.

It was odd that she didn't say anything to stop me. We talked about it later. Why Mrs Bernard Morton didn't say anything to stop me.

I put the car in gear and we were off.

It was only after we'd got to Maryhill Road that I turned my head and looked at her and thought, She's not a girl, which wasn't the way it was supposed to be. But then I wasn't a knight on horseback, either.

CHAPTER SEVEN

Mrs Morton and I went north in the end; but that was later and almost by accident.

The first parking place I found after I came to my senses, appalled at what I'd done, was in a side street off Queen Margaret Drive. I made a hash of reversing in and the nose of the car stuck out into the road as if pointing at the BBC sign on the building opposite. But when I garbled out some kind of an apology and started to get out of the car, she asked, 'Didn't he tell you to . . . ?'

Another first: that was the first time I heard her voice. It was deeper than I expected, though there was no reason for me to expect it to be any one thing rather than another. As it turned out, she had a cold. I liked it, that first voice, husky, a little deeper than I'd expected.

When I couldn't think of an answer, she panicked. Suddenly she was fighting for breath and saying over and over, 'My God, my God.'

'You can go back,' I said. On the other side of Queen Margaret Drive three birds flew up out of a tree in the Botanic Gardens. I ducked my head to the side to follow them up into the sky. Behind me the noises she made went on and on. The birds rose out of sight. 'Half an hour, twenty-five minutes. You can go back, and he won't even know you've gone.'

Without waiting for an answer, I got out and walked away. I crossed at the lights and went down Byres Road. My head was thumping and I went into the Curlers, the first pub I came to. I needed to sit by myself and think. Instead, as I stood at the counter this weird old guy started talking at me.

'I'm so glad to be able to piss again, son,' he said. 'A month ago I had a catheter in after the operation and I went back to hospital and couldn't piss. If you can't manage to piss, you get sent home again with it still bloody in. There were two of us trying that afternoon. He wasn't having any better luck than I was. "Tom," I said to him, when we were going off to have another go, "why is it this problem makes us walk like ducks?" "Oh, Billy," he says, "I always walk this way – I have a deformity." '

At that point I left. That's the way it is with friends. Win some, lose some, ships that pass in the night.

I walked at first and then found I was running. I ran all the way until I saw the car and then I went slowly, but it wasn't long before I could make her out, in the same seat, everything just the same. She hadn't moved.

I was so angry. I thought, Any man could make her sit in a car all day.

And then I was ashamed.

She wasn't crying any more, though, and I should have paid more attention to that, for when we got to the traffic lights she put her hand over mine on the wheel and pulled firmly. Taken by surprise, I turned left instead of right. I'd wanted to take her back to the factory, park the car where it had been, get out and leave her there, hope her husband hadn't looked out of the window and no one had noticed she'd gone. It wasn't much of a plan, but I wanted to make everything all right for her, the way it had been before.

Now we were going the wrong way, but I decided she wanted me to take her home, and I owed her that much. I could even imagine where we'd be going.

The Mortons would have the kind of house I'd seen pictures of in the paper, a big one in Giffnock, the kind of place someone who owned a factory would live in. We'd turn into a street of grey stone, detached houses; I'd jump out of the car and take off before she went in. 'Hello, dear, I'm home. The nice young man took me for a little drive.' I'd be stranded on the wrong side of the city, miles from anything familiar. As I tried to make my way back, I'd have to keep looking over my shoulder. Only thing was, Morton might not use this car to come after me. It could be anything. I might look round and see another car and next minute Bernard and his mates would be laying about me.

Working all that out kept me busy. Whenever I asked her for directions, she frowned and gave a little shake of her head, not as though refusing but as if my voice had taken her by surprise. By the time I noticed there were fields on both sides, it was too late: we were on our way to Edinburgh. It didn't seem like a choice at all, not for me. You couldn't say, either, that it was her decision. It was made somewhere between us, if it was made at all. That's what happens on that road if you don't turn right or left. All you have to do is keep on going.

CHAPTER EIGHT

I got trapped behind a lorry, then another, and cars kept passing me. This went on for miles until, just past the sign for Harthill, the road went to three lanes and, not realising the middle lane was for overtaking in both directions, I pulled out. A car came rushing at me head on. I stood on the brakes and just managed to squeeze back in. When I looked at Mrs Morton, her head had sagged forward as if she'd passed out. To tell the truth, having been given half a dozen lessons by the Hairy Bastard when he was still in a mood to impress my mother, at the best of times I wasn't all that wonderful a driver.

Clutching the wheel, staring ahead in shock, I heard myself being asked, 'My God, should you be driving?'

I'd swallowed a pint in the Curlers, I remembered, swallowed it too fast on an empty stomach, but I wasn't drunk.

'I'm fine,' I said.

'I mean, do you even have a licence?'

'I didn't know about the middle lane,' I said.

'What age are you?' Her voice wasn't loud, not much above a whisper, but it was calmer than I'd have expected.

Her question made me angry. My stomach was still in knots from the near miss. 'None of your business. You tell me.'

'My age?'

'Is it a secret?'

'Thirty-eight,' she said.

After a time, I said, 'I'm eighteen,' and she closed her eyes.

She opened them after a while, but she didn't speak until we were in the centre of Edinburgh.

'Can we stop?' she asked. 'Please?'

And that's what I did. I swung in to the pavement and stopped.

Speaking suddenly like that after so long a silence, she'd startled me. She'd seemed not even to notice the glances I'd stolen at her on the journey. As for me, not knowing whether she was thinking or lost in a dream world of her own, I hadn't known what to say to her. Now that the dam was breached, I braced myself for the long-delayed flood of questions and anger. If she'd called me crazy, I wouldn't have argued.

'We were driving round in circles.' She said it as if she felt I needed an explanation.

'I was looking for somewhere to park,' I said.

'Does it matter? One place or another?'

Before I could answer, she was out of the car. I had the door open before I remembered to switch off and take out the key.

Though it was only fifty miles from where I'd lived all my life, I'd never been in Edinburgh before. Despite the crowds on the pavement, I liked the sensation of space, the length of Princes Street ahead of us, on one side no buildings, just gardens and open sky above the castle on its rock. I felt excited and then I felt hungry. I glanced past Mrs Morton at the entrance to a department store. 'I need to eat,' I told her.

'It's late,' she said, sounding surprised. She started across the street as the lights changed, walking quickly – maybe she was hungry, too – and I followed her until we finished up in a place with cloths on the table.

When the waiter brought a menu I didn't even try to make sense of it. I'd never been in a restaurant before, never held a menu. I passed it across. If I'd altered her life, it seemed only fair that she got to order the meal.

I could hear myself eating the soup, it was quiet, murmur murmur murmur, nobody laughing or shouting. There wouldn't have been any trouble holding a conversation, if we could have thought of anything to say. Halfway through the soup, I noticed that she was using a different spoon. I checked at the next table and the one beyond, where they were using spoons like mine for eating ice cream and fruit. I had the illusion of an endless line of spoons and every time mine was the wrong one. I put the spoon in my mouth and sucked it, then licked under it. When I'd done that I put it back on the table and took the other one. As I did, I saw her watching a little smear I'd missed spread out as a stain on the white cloth. I felt the heat rise from my neck until my cheeks were burning.

The silence lasted until the waiter brought her main course, a big plate with slices of meat on it laid out like a fan. When he went away, I asked, 'What's that?'

'Aylesbury duckling,' she said.

I don't care what's wrong with it, I thought. Not much of a joke, but you have to try. I slid one of the little potatoes into my mouth. It was new and had flecks of green round it. The chicken was nice, too; but, if I'd been allowed only one or the other, I'd have taken the potatoes. I love potatoes.

'How much will all this cost?' I asked.

'I've no idea.'

I put another potato in and chewed on what it must be like to be able to buy something without checking the price tag.

'It's a different world,' I said to her.

'What is?'

'Your one.'

'I don't know what you mean.'

'I mean you could walk out into the street right now, go into the first shop, buy anything that took your fancy. You wouldn't have to look at what it cost.'

'Oh, dear,' she said and pushed her plate away.

What was ailing the duck? Alarmed, I thought she might expect me to call the waiter and complain.

'How silly of me,' she said. 'What was I thinking of?' I didn't know what, but the look on her face told me something was badly wrong. 'I wasn't thinking at all. The truth is I've stopped thinking. You're right, I have been in a different world.'

'I'm sorry if I upset you. It was just—'

'I don't have a handbag,' she said. 'I'm not carrying a handbag. Where would I have money?'

When she was here before, it would have been with her husband, so I'd been right in one way. What would it have mattered how expensive the place was? Mr Bernard was paying.

41

'I got my wage packet today.' She looked relieved. 'Have you any idea how much I got toiling for Mr Bernard for a week?'

Of course, she didn't know. 'Enough, surely, for dinner?'

'Not a lot' was the answer.

My turn to push the plate away, and there they sat, two plates almost touching in the middle of the table. I'd left more than half and she'd hardly started on hers. Clearing the plates wouldn't have cost any more; leaving most of it didn't save a penny. For two hungry people we were being pretty stupid.

CHAPTER NINE

As if I was trying to prove something, when we got back to the car I got behind the wheel. She looked at me, but didn't say anything.

We went up Lothian Road and then through Morningside. I knew that because Mrs Morton named the streets as she told me to turn left and right.

'And petrol.' I was just talking, saying things as they came into my head. 'We haven't got money for petrol.' At the top of the second hill, I read the sign and checked with her, 'Is this the fastest way back to Glasgow? Have we got enough petrol?'

I wasn't happy about what would be waiting for me there, but we didn't have any choice but to go back. People were waiting for us. You could say we were overdue.

We weren't more than half an hour on the road when the range of hills on our right began to fade as light drained from the sky. We didn't have anything to say to each other, yet I wanted to talk to her. I wanted to tell her I had never intended to do her this harm. I wanted to tell her who I was. I wanted to tell her I was sorry. It didn't matter. I couldn't find words for any of it. The funny thing is at the same time I was conscious of how my foot easing up and down changed the note of the engine, and of the road ahead like a grey silk ribbon unspooling from the wheel between my hands. I was coping, and it felt good.

It was Mrs Morton who took fright. 'You can't drive like this. Put on the lights'; and when I couldn't find them and we had to stop (pulling in side-on by a farm gate), she opened the door of the car and was going to get out until, having found them, I put the lights off again and agreed we'd wait there until morning.

'If that's what you want.' Stupid bloody woman.

While I was sulking, she suddenly sank back away from me, so that she was almost lying down. There must have been a lever or button to adjust the seat like that, and if I'd felt around I suppose I'd have found one for my seat, but that didn't seem right and so I sat staring out of the window as night fell. It was dark in the car.

'I'm sorry,' I said.

She didn't say anything, but I could tell by her breathing she was awake.

'If it would help, I'll talk to your husband, tell him I take the blame. I got in the car and drove it away. What could you do to stop me?'

A car came towards us on main beam. When it had passed, I could see stars of yellow light on the dark.

'Scream?' she asked. 'Throw open the door and jump out?'

'You thought he'd sent me. That's why you let it happen.'

'An eighteen-year-old boy? I doubt he'd believe that.'

'That's what you told me.'

'I don't know . . .' Her voice trailed off. 'So why am I still here?'

'Any way I can make things better. Just tell me what I should do.'

'And why didn't I ask for help in the restaurant? He could ask that as well.'

'Tell him you were afraid of me.'

'You're not very frightening,' she said.

I flared up like a match thrown in a pool of oil. 'And I can't drive,' I said. 'And no, if you want the truth, I don't have a licence.' As soon as the words left my mouth, I heard them as stupid. Miserably, I finished, 'I don't even know which bloody spoon to eat soup with.'

After a silence, she sighed and said, 'Once at college I made a friend and asked her home for dinner. She wasn't sure about coming. We lived in a big house in Bearsden and she came from a poor background. I don't know what she expected, I don't know what I expected, I never brought friends home.'

Through the windscreen, I could see the curve of a hill, with the sky lighter above it and a scatter of stars endlessly signalling. I didn't look down, but all the time and now more than ever I was conscious of her legs and body solid among the shadows.

'All through the meal my father talked about this problem at work – he was an engineer – and gradually I saw this girl losing all her shyness and just sitting wondering what the hell was going on. When it was over, I started to clear away the dishes. "I'll lend a hand," she said. "Well," my father said, "I hope you make a better job of it than Mother and Eileen. I have to supervise to make sure it is done as it should be done." In the kitchen, we laid everything out, knives, forks, the different kinds of spoons, and then the plates, the bowls, the cups. My friend said, "Can I say how we'd do them at home? We wash all the cleaner ones first and then, when the water gets dirty, we wash the worst off the dirty plates and run clean water to finish them off." Doing dishes didn't interest me, but it seemed logical. My father shook his head and smiled and said, "This will give you the opportunity to see how it should be done." Somebody told me – there's always somebody to tell you, isn't there? – that she swore to everybody next day she'd just met the most boring man in the world. After that, we weren't friends any more.'

I listened and kept listening until her breathing slowed and it seemed she slept. Every so often an approaching car would flood the interior with light, making me feel exposed and vulnerable. As the hours crawled by, I envied her.

My first thought was that I must have slept after all, for the sky was pale and a watery sun sat on top of low clouds. My second thought was that Mrs Morton's leg was touching mine. She was sprawled on her back and her mouth lay open a little. It was as if I was seeing her for the first time. She looked as if she didn't have a care in the world. I felt her warmth and moved gently away, my breath loud in my ears.

I eased the door of the car shut. A cow resting her head on top of the gate stared at me with big brown eyes. As far as I knew, a cow wasn't a ferocious beast, but then I hadn't ever been this close to one. With a full bladder, getting back in the car wasn't an option. I needed a few minutes of privacy. When I climbed the gate, the cow didn't move, but as I swung my leg over and jumped down she skittered away, stopping after a dozen steps to look back at me. As I started to walk up the field, she slowly followed me and then I realised a dozen others were taking an interest. Each one paused now and then to take a mouthful of grass, but all tended in the same direction, drifting towards me like sticks in a stream. By now, though, as I came up the field I had a better view of what looked like a tower on top of the hill.

When I got closer, I saw that the stones of it were unshaped and irregular. It seemed to me that it must be very old. There was an opening in the side and I went in and then saw the stair. It wound up in the thickness of the wall, and I started to climb, thinking there would be a barrier at the first turn, but the rough irregular steps led all the way to the top. I came out on a walkway and the air smelled of the early morning as I ventured round it. The stone path was wide enough to be safe, but the parapet on the outside only came up to my knees and the one on the inside was missing in places. All the way up the field I'd had an erection, but it softened as I peed through one of the gaps. I watched the flow curve out and fray as it fell into the shadow down towards the broken stones and grass. A little breeze blew in my face and I felt good. 'Top of the world, Ma!'

As I was tucking myself away, I heard voices. My elation evaporated. With the instincts of an intruder, I headed back to the opening, stepping very lightly so that my footsteps wouldn't echo on the stone. I went in the same fashion down the stairs, hurrying into the open as if escaping from a trap.

It was a relief to see the empty slope of field and the scatter of grazing cows. Telling myself I'd mistaken crows or sheep or whatever for voices, I walked along by the wall to make sure. And there they were. Two of them, father and son by the look of them, with their heads thrown back gazing up at the top of the tower. My first thought was that they couldn't have seen me up there. This close, all you saw was cloud pouring like water across the lip of the parapet. The old man turned his head, just his head, still thrown back, to look at me. Hairs sprouted from his nose and his mouth hung open so that I could see there were as many gaps as blackened teeth. He gave a little grunt and the son's head swung to me every bit as slowly. Their look was considering, the look of people who had a right to be there this early in the morning. Both sets of eyes were brown, cow-eye colour, the colour of the beasts they owned.

The resemblance, though, ended there. Unlike farmer and son, cows didn't carry thick sticks. Their mild brown eyes hadn't between one instant and the next flushed red.

I ran down the field with my breath roaring in my ears. Two of the cattle got in my way, and dashing between them my feet almost slid from under me. All the way, I heard the old man yelling as if he was demented, 'Hit him! Catch him and hit him!'

By the time I got to the gate, there was nothing to do but smack both hands on the top bar and jump. Hard enough to take my head off, a stick clanged on the gate as I landed.

I scrambled in through the open door of the car and fell back in the passenger seat as Mrs Morton put her foot down and the car shot out into the road.

It took time to get my breath back. My cheeks were wet, as if I might have wept.

At last I said, 'You can drive. I didn't know if you could.'

She wrinkled her nose. 'Did you step in something?'

I wondered for a nasty moment what she meant, but when I turned up my shoe the smear across the sole was just cow shite.

CHAPTER TEN

'Where are we going?' I asked.
  The question had been a long time coming. We'd gone for hours and miles in silence. At Uddingston, we were almost back into Glasgow.

'Home,' she said.

'But it's early.' Stupid thing to say.

She understood me, though. 'The factory? Is that where I should be? Sitting outside the factory?'

We went through Cambuslang, Burnside, Kingspark. I watched the names of the streets go by. I wasn't sure what roads would take us to the factory, but that's where I wished she would go. I wanted to wind time back for her and make everything all right.

In a street of shops, I asked, 'Could you stop here?'

When she pulled in, she didn't switch off the engine. I listened to it and watched the people going by. The sun was shining; you'd have thought someone would be smiling.

'It's your car,' I told her. 'Go where you want. I'll get out.'

She turned to look at me. I don't mean just her head. She twisted round from the shoulders to get a good look at me.

'Like you did before.'

It took me a moment to work it out. She meant the day before, that's all it was, only the day before, outside the BBC in Queen Margaret Drive.

'That's right.' I mean, Christ! why not?

'You came back then. Why did you do that?'

I thought about it and lied. 'I was drunk,' I said.

'No. You weren't.'

'Because I was stupid?'

It wasn't easy to bring back the image of the look she'd given me when I said I'd get out and leave her, for it had gone almost as soon as it came, so quickly it would have been easy to believe I'd imagined it. Yet I wouldn't have been sorry to see it back again. Being looked at as if I'd crawled out from under a stone was better than the blank nothingness of her expression now; you could have carved it out of ice.

'Would you tell me one thing before you go?' she asked. 'Why did you drive the car away?'

Another question that had been a long time coming.

For want of any better answer, I told her about the week's lying time and how her husband, Mr Bernard, had fired me.

She looked at me in disbelief. 'That was all?'

That and having no future and no home.

'He called me Mr Gas,' I offered.

CHAPTER ELEVEN

I didn't get out of the car. Apart from being fired and the contempt of Mr Bernard, some image of a knight, some absurd notion of rescue, had been part of the crazy impulse that had got us into this mess, though I couldn't imagine ever admitting it. For whatever reason of her own, she didn't question my staying. She didn't take us to the factory, though, perhaps not wanting to put my courage to the test.

I'd been right about one thing. Grey stone, bow windows, the Mortons lived in just the kind of house I'd imagined for her. The gates were open and she took the car into the drive, pulled up close to the garage and switched off. Here at the side of the house it was quiet. The garage doors were wood with four little windowpanes on either side at the top. You'd think someone with a factory would have a metal door on his garage. One of the glass panes was cracked. I listened to the engine ticking as it cooled, and thought surely now had to be the time to jump out and run for it. A goodbye speech, so far as I could see, wouldn't be expected.

'Have you any money?' she asked.

'What?'

'No, of course you haven't. I'll find something.' I stared at her. 'You can't just wander off without a penny.' She opened the door and started to get out. 'Don't worry, he won't be here.'

The hall was long and narrow and, when my eyes adjusted to the dimness after the sunshine outside, I saw a stair going up and another that curled in a tight spiral down into the gloom of what must have been a basement. I leaned on the rail and peered down, but the stairs went out of sight before they got to whatever was down there. I took a couple of steps down, changed my mind and came up. I wandered from one end of the hall to the other and stood looking up to the first-floor landing. Whatever she was doing up there, she was taking her time. I imagined her rummaging through a drawer for a purse, the way she might to pay the milkman. Maybe she was trying to decide how much, putting some of the coins back. Tired of thinking that way, I opened a door and the room beyond was flooded with sunshine.

There was a table covered in papers, so big it filled the whole middle of the floor, and glass doors on the far wall. Though it was the ground floor, there was a balcony beyond the glass and I could see the tops of trees. A folded partition at the back gave a view into a second room with fat dark leather chairs you'd sink into, and beside them little tables with mats. An arch opened on to a third space with a desk and a wall lined with shelves crammed with books. Curiosity made me go in to see what kind of books they were, and I was reading the titles when her voice behind me said, 'Oh, this is where you are, then.'

'I wasn't touching anything.'

'The books belonged to his father. Bernard's not much of a reader.'

'Nice.' Nice, all the same, I meant; nice to have so many. 'You'd never be short of something to read.'

She frowned at the shelves. 'I never saw Papa Morton with a book. He had his stroke just before I met Bernard. After we were married, everyone took it for granted I'd look after him, maybe because I'd been a nurse. I came back from my honeymoon to this house.'

'It's a nice house,' I said. What did I imagine I was trying to tell her? That she'd done well for herself? What did I know? I was only eighteen. The good thing was that she didn't pay any attention. Still frowning at the shelves, she might not even have heard me.

'The first time I saw him lying in bed he seemed old to me, but that's because I was young. He was only in his fifties. It was years before he died.'

Afterwards she gave me money and I took it. I stood in the street outside her gate and told myself I'd taken it because I didn't know what else to do, and I went over ways I might have refused, gracefully so that she would have been impressed; and then I thought, No, you took it because you had no money and it's a long way to walk home.

And after all when it came to it I did go on foot half across the city. I walked because before anything else I had to get to a main road; and then I walked because I wasn't tired. As I walked from one stop to another, I checked the route numbers for the buses and trams. They went by me halfway between one stop and the next. I couldn't be bothered joining a queue to wait, walking was nothing to me. At last, I came to a stop and people were getting on a bus. I'd walked past it before I glanced up and saw its destination; and then I got on as if that was what I'd been waiting for.

CHAPTER TWELVE

I walked by the factory gate twice, the second time all the way to the corner where I could see the bus stop. While I stood, a bus came. It would have taken a good run to catch it, but maybe the driver would have waited for me; some drivers did. I watched it go, then returned to the gate and this time went in, not giving myself time to think. I was back where I had begun a week ago.

I'd assumed I'd have to talk my way upstairs, but there wasn't anyone behind the counter. Dully, from behind the door that led to the factory, machinery clattered. Saturday was a working day. A phone rang somewhere through in the back and when it stopped I heard the murmur of a woman's voice answering. Maybe the receptionist had gone somewhere quieter to practise her sneer. I took the stairs two at a time before I lost my nerve.

The left-hand door lay open and I could see a filing cabinet with folders lying on top and one of the drawers pulled out. The middle door was Mr Bernard's. I knocked and waited. I mean, there wasn't any question of me bursting in. It was my hope that this was going to be a pretty low-key and civilised discussion. I knocked again and a voice inside made a noise that might have been 'Come in'.

The man behind the desk had his nose in a pile of papers. When he looked up, I recognised the fat bookkeeper. 'Yes?' he said vaguely. Behind the thick glasses, his eyes looked unfocused, as if he was still absorbed in a column of figures. He shoved fingers through hair already standing on end.

'I wanted to see Mr Morton.'

'So? Can I help you?'

'No.' I started to move back out of the room.

'Wait!' The high-pitched voice soared into a bat squeak that stopped me in my tracks. 'What makes you assume – Anything to do with this business, I can deal with it. You understand? Any . . . single . . . thing.'

If there's anything I hate, it's having an idea spelled out to me one word at a time. A teacher's trick that says, If I speak any faster, someone like you will be too stupid to take it in.

'It isn't about work,' I told him.

He shook his head as if he didn't believe me. 'Don't you know who I am?' He gave a flap of the hand, which looked petulant except that when the tips of his fingers hit the desk they hit it hard.

'I wasn't here for long,' I said. One week paid for in cash; thanks to him, come to think of it.

Then he did a funny thing. He looked down at the desk again and began tidying the papers he'd been working on. 'Give me a minute,' he said, which kept me there. He squared the pile, tapping it at the sides and top and bottom. He had big, puffy hands with fingers swollen as if they had too much blood pumped into them. He pushed the papers to one side so that the desk in front of him was clear, and when he looked up I saw that he had recognised me.

'What have you done with her?'

I stared at him. It hadn't occurred to me that the whole factory would know what had happened.

'Is Mr Morton here?'

'You can talk to me.' When I didn't answer, he said, 'He's not here.'

'Has he gone home?' The edge of panic in my voice surprised me.

'Is that where Eileen is?'

'Eileen?'

'Bernard's wife,' he said impatiently.

Then I remembered her story about her father organising the washing of the dishes. 'Eileen and Mother', she'd remembered him saying – and that was how I'd learned Mrs Morton's first name.

'What happened yesterday? What did she say to you? Did she ask you to take her away? You can tell me.'

I shook my head. It was what I had come to explain, that it was all my fault, but not to him.

'I'm Mr Norman, Mr Bernard's older brother.'

Fine, I'd call him in evidence. He could tell his brother that I hadn't even known her name.

'Where has she been all this time?' he asked.

'Nowhere.'

'Nowhere all night?'

'We slept in the car.'

'The two of you?' Disbelief puffed out his cheeks in a long breath. 'She's gone off her head. Where was this?'

'On the way back from Edinburgh.'

He threw up his hands as if to fend off any more. 'But now she's at home?' I nodded. 'What are you here for?'

'I wanted to tell Mr Bernard his wife didn't do anything wrong. I drove the car away. She couldn't stop me. He shouldn't blame her. Where is he?'

'Not here.' I took it that meant Mr Bernard had gone home. Before I could say anything, he asked, 'What made you steal the car?'

I was so worked up I didn't hear him properly. I blundered on. 'It was all my fault. From the minute I got into the car she kept saying, "Go back, go back!" But I wouldn't.'

'Why did you take it? You must have had a reason.'

'I didn't care about the car,' I said.

'Why take it, then?' But as he waited I couldn't think of any reason he would understand. 'Have you brought it back?'

'To the factory? What for?' I wasn't trying to upset him. I honestly couldn't imagine what he was talking about.

'So that my brother won't charge you with theft. He might not – not if you've brought it back.' It hadn't even occurred to me that I could be charged with some crime. I hadn't stolen anything. 'You'd have nothing to worry about if you've brought it back.'

'It's at the house.' Little bookkeeper! Fuck the car, I thought. 'Your brother won't be worrying about the car,' I told him.

He shook his head at me and gave a little sigh.

CHAPTER THIRTEEN

There was a time when I started going to church and the minister, Mr Peters, listened when I finally got up courage to ask him about finding my father and said he'd think about it and let me know. On the way back to Mr Bernard's house, I remembered Mr Peters because the only time he ever gave me a lift I was terrified. He jumped lights and went too fast and cut in on other drivers, shaking his fist and calling them fools. Who would have thought a minister would drive like a crazy man? That was exactly the way Norman Morton drove, fat hands clutching the wheel, except that he called other drivers cunts instead of fools.

Reverend Peters didn't swear. On the other hand, he never did get back to me on how to find someone in a big city. After a few months I stopped going to church. And if some day my father got round to sending another card, I wouldn't ever know, not now I'd left home.

Norman took us into Bernard's drive so fast I thought he might carry one of the stone gateposts along for company. Then I remembered Mrs Morton saying this house had belonged to Bernard's father. If it was the family home, Norman had been brought up here, too, and might have missed that gatepost by an inch a thousand times before.

He tried to open the garage, but it was locked. 'If she's come back, where's the car?' He peered in between the doors. 'Can't see a thing.'

'Why don't you just go and ring the bell?'

He spat on one of the glass panes and got up on tiptoe to rub it with the edge of his hand. 'See if it's there!' he ordered and, when I hesitated, gestured at me to do as I was told.

I wondered if he was trying to delay going to the door. It was an unpleasant idea. If the fat man was afraid of his brother, how afraid should I be?

Maybe he was afraid of what we might find when we went inside. An even more unpleasant idea.

'What are you waiting for?' Norman squeaked.

Because I was taller, it was easier for me to look inside. I tried each pane in turn. It made no difference. There was paint or something on the inside of the glass.

I shook my head at him and without waiting for his reaction went over to the front door. I pressed the button and the bell shrilled inside. The bow windows were shrouded in net curtains. It wasn't a house that gave anything away.

'Maybe she's sleeping,' Norman said.

He reached round as if he was scratching his rump, and after a bit of effort produced a flat brown wallet. When he opened it, there were keys of different lengths hung from a bar. I recognised it. His car keys were there, and the wallet had dangled from the ignition as he drove.

'You've got a key for the house?' I'm not saying it was a brilliant deduction.

'Why not?' He put it into the lock. 'Bernard has a key for my flat.'

I wondered how Mrs Morton felt about him having a key to her house. I wished I knew where she was. I was worried about her.

The hall was dark, the way it had been the first time. All the doors off it were closed. Norman leaned on the banister and stared down into the blackness at the foot of the spiral stair. When he went down, I went after him. He turned and looked at me but didn't say anything. There was a little passage that led to a big room with ovens and sinks and work surfaces and cupboards and a long wooden table with chairs round it. You could see trees and flowerbeds outside. It wasn't gloomy the way I'd imagined.

He told me to stay where I was and went back upstairs, moving surprisingly lightly, the way some fat men do. It was his brother's house. And I was nobody. Walking round his factory, he wouldn't see me, I wouldn't register, a kid pushing a dump cart. He'd every right to tell me to stay put. And I resented it like hell.

I tried to picture the outside of the house. The ground floor was above me, but was there one floor above that or two? If I heard her voice, I'd go up. What else could I do, even if she didn't want me to? I stood at the foot of the stairs, straining to listen. Silence, I couldn't hear a thing, but it was a big house. Anything could be happening. And then I got it into my head Bernard might have come home and she might be lying up there unconscious. I knew that was being stupid. A house like this, people wouldn't behave like that, I told myself. All the same, I could see fat Norman peering in through the door of a bedroom where he'd found her lying on the floor. At once, I imagined him coming down with some excuse to get rid of me. Once I was gone, he'd climb back upstairs and crouch, panting, like he'd done in front of the filing cabinet in the office, his fat belly hanging over her.

With my head full of what I'd imagined, I climbed the spiral stair, went along the hall and started up one slow step at a time towards the first floor until I was halfway and could see a table with a blue vase and a strip above it of a picture. A painting, I mean, like the ones in the galleries at Kelvingrove, where Tony and I sometimes went on a Saturday to look at the marine engines and the stuffed animals and room after room of paintings.

Apart from the ticking of a clock, there wasn't a sound, no cries for help, nothing like that. I didn't have the nerve to go up even as far as where the painting was.

Retreating to the dark hall, I remembered how only a couple of hours ago I'd stood here waiting for Mrs Morton to find some money to give me.

I opened the door I'd opened then, knowing I'd see a view of the front room and a balcony looking on to trees in the garden and an arched entry through to where the books were. And just as I turned the handle and walked in, it came to me Bernard was going to be there.

It was just as I remembered: partitions folded back; front room lit by the sun as if it was set up on a stage; the long table with a magazine laid open as if it had been put down a moment ago. I'd got it all right, except that it wasn't Bernard at the desk inside the arch. It was Mrs Morton.

Elbows either side of the phone, she was leaning forward resting her chin and mouth against folded hands. The position might have made it seem she was staring into the garden, but she was so intent I doubted if she was aware of anything but her own thoughts. Could she have been phoning? Was there anyone she could turn to for help?

At Norman's voice sounding through the hall, she turned her head and saw me.

Before she could say anything, Norman called behind me, 'Get out of there. Have you touched anything?'

As I turned, he saw her and lost interest in me. 'I've been all over the house looking for you,' he cried.

'I was here.'

'If you heard me, you should have called, let me know where you were hiding. What the hell do you think you're playing at?'

I didn't like the way he spoke to her, without any respect at all.

'Bernard isn't here, Norman,' she said. Not 'My husband isn't here, so what are you doing walking into my house, you fat bastard?'

He gaped at her. 'Of course he isn't.' He looked at me. 'This is private. Wait through there. Out in the hall.'

When I hesitated, he reached for my arm.

'Don't fucking touch me,' I said. And then, like a fool, I said to her, 'Why do you let him talk to you like that?' As if it was any of my business.

She rubbed her forehead in a gesture between distress and trying to think. 'You shouldn't have come back. I want you to go.'

'Not till I'm sure you're all right.'

'I will be. Please.' She gestured as if pushing me away. 'I don't know why you're here.'

'I've been to the factory. I wanted to tell your husband you weren't to blame. But he wasn't there.'

She stared at me in fright. 'Why would you do that?'

At the question, spoken with a kind of bewilderment, Norman lost patience. 'Oh, Christ!' he exclaimed.

As he blundered towards the desk, I shouted, 'Don't touch her!'

The noise of it swung him round. 'What? Don't what? Me?' 'Just don't touch her!'

'Oh, God!' he said. Unbelievable, he meant, and just as quickly as that he was in control of himself again. To me he said, 'I don't know what kind of tinker camp you came out of, but this is a civilised house with civilised people in it.' To her, with a big gusty sigh, he complained softly and reasonably, 'How could he get such nonsense into his head?' And when she didn't answer at once, 'What on earth have you been saying to him?'

She was looking down at a bowl with flowers to the side of the desk, and didn't raise her head. The flowers were bent over with brown petals. 'Poor things,' she said. 'They've been neglected.'

'Flowers?' And with the word he looked at me – Jesus, man to man – in astonishment at her stupidity. 'Never mind bloody flowers. Where's the key of the garage?'

'She didn't have to say anything to me,' I told him. 'Don't you think everybody in the factory knows? He makes her sit outside all day. What kind of bastard would do that?'

What upset me was that he didn't show any anger now, just bit his lip and shook his head as it might be pityingly. 'Oh, Eileen,' he said, 'Eileen. Let's get rid of this boy. Start by telling him no one's ever – my brother would never – lay a finger on you. Isn't that true?'

'If she said that, I wouldn't believe her.' Pushing in before she could say a word, not letting her speak for herself. Taking my cue from him, you could say; and so no better than he was.

'You know nothing about her,' he said. 'You don't know about Alice.'

'He's talking about my dead baby,' Mrs Morton said.

He looked surprised, perhaps because she'd spoken quietly, without any show of emotion. Without having it explained to me, I understood it hadn't been like that with her before.

Perhaps, altogether apart from her tone, he had never heard her simply say what had happened until that moment, acknowledge her child's death in that way, as a fact like every other.

She swept up the dry leaves round the bowl and poured them out of her hand on to the dusty earth.

'When she died I was ill,' she said quietly, 'and after that things were different.'

'What are you explaining to him for?' he asked, although he had started it. 'Family business,' he told me. 'You shouldn't even be here.'

It was hard to find an argument against that. While I was trying to think of one, Mrs Morton said, 'The car isn't in the garage.'

'Eh?'

'You asked for the key of the garage. I thought you wanted the car for some reason.'

'If it's not in the garage—'

'It broke down.' She glanced at me. 'I took it to the shops. I had to get a taxi home.'

'Broke down where? My God, you left it in the street?'

'No. It's in Howie's. I phoned them when I got home and they sent a tow truck to fetch it. They'll check it over and let Bernard know what's wrong.'

'Howie's? The one in Morris Street?'

'That's right.'

And at once he wanted to leave. He wasn't in such a hurry, though, that he didn't want me out of there first. It was a shock to him when Mrs Morton said no, she would phone for a taxi to take me home. Later on it would occur to me that was a brave thing for her to do. I mean that I thought in the way her life had shaped itself in that house, there must have been a mass of things she wasn't allowed to do, which was a disgusting thought and one I'd rather not have had. There are thoughts like that; they come from nowhere and breed in your head like maggots in the dark if you let them. He dithered and blustered, but she phoned anyway.

'Ten minutes,' she said putting the phone down.

I thought he'd wait, but he was off almost at once.

She went through to the front room and watched at the window. As I followed her, I heard his car start up. After a moment, she turned and said, 'We'd better get out of here before he gets back.'

'Back from where?'

'Howie's. Didn't you have the impression that's where he was going?'

'What makes you think he'll come back?'

'Because the car isn't in Howie's,' she said. 'I parked it in the lane at the back of the house.'

CHAPTER FOURTEEN

S he had to explain it to me: that she hadn't phoned a taxi, but had pressed numbers at random and spoken over the voice of a woman who, after telling her twice she'd a wrong number, asked if she was deaf and hung up.

'I can find the scheme,' she said, 'but once we're there you'll have to guide me to the house.'

She was taking me home, that's what she called it, meaning the house Alec Turner lived in with his new girlfriend. Before I could ask why, she told me about the phone call she'd taken just before Norman and I arrived at the house. 'Whoever it was didn't know your name,' she said, and broke off.

'Harry Glass,' I said.

If she'd given her name in return, I could have said, 'Pleased to meet you'; except that I already knew her name and hadn't anything to be pleased about.

'Or where you lived,' she said. 'That's what he was phoning to find out.'

The man had called just after I left, wanting to speak to Bernard. As soon, however, as he'd realised who she was, he started asking what had happened to her and where had she been.

'It must be somebody from the factory,' I said. 'The whole place seems to know about yesterday.'

She frowned doubtfully. 'Anyone from the factory would have asked for Bernard differently. There wasn't any respect. And, apart from that, I've never heard a voice like that before, such a strange voice.'

'Strange?'

She hesitated. 'A . . . A kind of rough whisper.'

'Maybe he had a cold.'

63

She gave me a look and, no, I didn't think so, either. Something about that voice had frightened her, so much so that she'd hidden the car in the lane at the back of the house because she'd told him I'd driven off in it after taking her home.

Fuck's sake.

'Why did you do that? What was the point of saying that to him? That was a lie.' I heard myself babbling and made the effort to stop.

'He asked if the car was here,' she said. 'Why would he ask that? I couldn't make sense of it, but I didn't want him coming to the house. And then, in case he came anyway, I hid it in the lane.'

There had been no explicit threats, only the persistence of the questioning, but something in the voice had made her afraid. Yet, despite being frightened, now she wanted to take me home. Bad conscience, I suppose, but it was brave of her. It was maybe part of the change that had made her defy Norman back there in the house, something I'd have laid a bet she wouldn't have done before I'd kidnapped her and ruined her life. The jury had to be out on how badly.

As for me, I sat there and was too ashamed to tell her we were going to a place I'd been thrown out of and where there was no one I cared about or who cared for me. I couldn't do it, and while we went out of Giffnock and across town until we came to the tenements of Maryhill, and then up past Springburn and out into the familiar wasteland of pebbledash houses, I drifted into a plan. I'd let her take me home and once she'd driven off I'd walk away. Where to, God alone knew, but leave the hard questions for later. One good thing: I wasn't worried about her mystery man on the phone. After all, he didn't know where I lived; and how could he get my address, when he didn't even know my name?

We drove past the row of half a dozen shops opposite the scrubland where legend had it they planned to put a cinema some day; and up the hill to arrive at last outside the Hairy Bastard's mansion – easily recognisable by the size of the weeds in the side garden.

Mrs Morton sat looking at it for a while. 'This is where you live?' she asked at last.

'The garden looked better when my father was here,' I said. My father, of course, had never even seen the place. It seemed I couldn't stop telling lies to her.

'I'm sorry.' I realised she thought he was dead. 'Do you live here with your mother?'

'You don't want to hear my life story.' I opened the door. 'Thanks for the lift.'

I got out – and then thought that, all things considered, she'd been pretty decent, and tried to find something better to say as a farewell, but being a slow thinker was still bent over looking in at her when the wailing started. It came from inside the house and it lasted for only a moment, but I felt the hairs go up on the back of my neck.

'Oh, my God,' Mrs Morton said. Next moment she was out of the car. I followed her up the path and watched as she rang the bell, waited, and rang again. I gathered her idea was that we should check if anything was wrong.

I still had my key and unfortunately he hadn't changed the lock. Maybe he was saving that for when he went off on holiday, in case I came back and held a trash party for a few hundred guests.

In the hall it was so quiet I could hear Mrs Morton behind me panting softly as if she'd been running. Listening to her, it came clear in my mind how bad an idea it had been to borrow Mr Bernard's wife. Never mind the mystery man who had phoned her, Mr Morton frightened me. It was a bit late to realise that, but as I said I'm a slow thinker.

'Who's there?' Any higher and I'd have been squeaking like a bat.

Nothing happened for all of half a minute and then the phone rang.

I reached out and picked it up without thinking. I'd lived there long enough, I didn't have to look. The Hairy Bastard had put it in. I knew where we kept the phone.

'Alec?' I said.

But it wasn't him.

A woman's voice asked, 'Is that Harry Glass?'

Fighting down an instinct to deny it, I grunted.

'This is Theresa. You took Mr Bernard's car key off my desk. It was you, wasn't it?' I didn't answer. When she got tired of waiting, she asked, 'Are you still there?' I cleared my throat. 'You hadn't any right to do that. I got into terrible trouble.'

'Sorry,' I said.

There was a pause. Mrs Morton was in front of me, trying to catch my eye. I looked away.

The voice in my ear said, 'I'm sorry, too.'

'What?'

'I shouldn't have given him your name and address. I've been worrying about it all morning. But Mr Bernard wasn't there and he didn't want to speak to Mr Norman. So I got out your form and told him, but I shouldn't have.'

'I don't understand. Who was it?'

'A friend of Mr Bernard's – that's all he said. "It's about the boy who took the car," he said. "I'm a friend of Bernard's."'

'You gave him my name and—'

'I knew it was wrong. Giving away company information, I'm trained not to do that.' Her voice was thin and apologetic. I could hardly fit it to the arrogant girl behind the reception desk at the factory.

'What did he look like?'

'That's the thing, it was over the phone. I don't understand how I could have been bullied by a voice on the phone. That's why I had to tell you. Just in case he . . . I've never done anything like that before. I am sorry.'

Behind Mrs Morton, the door of the front room was opening stealthily, an inch at a time. Nothing happened for all of half a minute and then a face came round the edge of the door. The first thing I saw was orange hair, a spike at a time, and then half of a wee pale face with eyes like raisins pissed into a snow bank.

At this point, Mrs Morton, registering something was wrong, turned round. 'Hello,' she said. 'You must be Harry's sister.'

It was kind of disgusting to realise the Hairy Bastard's new true love was about sixteen. But before I could ask her if she'd a home to go to, or was it so bad even cohabiting with a monkey was preferable, she took an unexpected initiative by calling me a cunt.

This took me aback. I was reminded of a guy at school who'd passed a crowd of Celtic supporters chanting, 'We are thu peepul,' and thought, not in anything but honest surprise – he being a follower of the late King Billy of Orange: No, you've got that wrong, *we* are. Which took me back to wee Spiky Head – the cunt of the first part, as it were.

'I don't think we've ever met,' I said, and at the response in my ear put the phone down.

'Aye, but I know you. You're Harry Glass.'

'Well, you've got that right.'

'It's because of you he's in hospital.'

'Who? Alec? Alec's in hospital?'

'Smashed up he is.'

'I'm sorry.' And in a funny way I was; I've always had a soft spot for animals. 'Did he get run over?'

'He got a battering. Because of you, ya—'

'Right, I heard you the first time. But you've got it wrong. Nothing to do with me.'

'It was you they came to the door asking for.'

'If he told you that, he was kidding you.' That's what I wanted to believe. After all, nobody liked Alec Turner. Chances were, he'd owed somebody money, or he'd got into a stupid argument, or else he'd been so pissed he'd taken a header down a flight of stairs. It was even possible wee Spiky Head had a couple of big brothers who'd caught up with him.

'I heard them myself when they came to the door. He opened it and the guy said, "Where's Harry?" and Alec said, "How the fuck would I know?" and next thing two of them were battering him the length of the lobby. They were just pure mental.'

I didn't decide to panic, it just happened. Questions steamed around in my head. I got one out. 'What else did they say?'

'How would I know? They took him through there and then the big one came out and picked me up and took me through and dropped me on the bed. I thought . . . you know. But he said, "Not a move out of you," and he put the blankets over my head. I lay there for ages and then the front door banged shut. Even then I lay for a while. I was awful frightened. Then I heard Alec groaning. I got out from under the blanket and he was trying to crawl in the door.'

'What did he say? Did he tell you what it was about?'

'He couldn't talk.'

I felt sick.

'I just sat beside him crying. Then I saw Mrs Fleming going to the shops and I shouted her. It was her sent for the police. I told them about you, they'll be looking for you. They're not long away.'

CHAPTER FIFTEEN

I've never liked hospitals much. One time my father was sick and my mother and I visited him; this would be when I was six or seven. He was in for about five weeks and we went two or three times a week. Saturday or Sunday was fine, because the tinkers didn't bother us at the weekend, I can't remember why, maybe because there were more folk visiting then. But through the week we'd get off the bus and we had to walk up this road past a field where there was a bunch of tinks camped. They'd come out and ask for cigarettes and once they threw stones at us. Maybe through the week we got a different bus. That would be it: from the shop where she worked. Anyway, six years old, I felt as if I should protect her. We were always glad to get past.

The neighbour, Mrs Fleming, had told me not only the hospital but that Alec Turner was in intensive care. One of the world's Samaritans, she'd rung to see how he was. 'The nurse said, holding his own.'

He looked as if he'd been dropped off a roof. His nose was taped and when I bent close what came out was this little voice full of spittle and slush and a whistle of broken teeth: 'What have you done?'

I'd expected him to curse me. Coming to the side of the bed, I'd been conscious of his one showing eye fixed on me like an evil spell.

'Nothing.'

'They wouldn't believe I didn't know where you were. "I'm not his fucking father," I told them. But they just kept on. They thought I was protecting you.'

I shook my head. Crazy. They might be good at handing out a hiding, but for sure they were no judges of character.

'I haven't done anything to get somebody after me,' I lied.

He shut his good eye and I thought he'd drifted off to sleep. But it opened abruptly and he whistled, 'They think you have.'

'Did they say who they were?'

'Oh, aye. Stuck a visiting card up my arse. You want to have a look for it?'

'Maybe the police'll find them.'

'Don't be stupid.' He wasn't a great believer in the police.

'I'm sorry about this. But it's nothing to do with me.'

I started to get up. He said something, but his speech was getting worse. I leaned close again.

'Did you steal a car? They want it back awful bad.'

I was at the door, when he made another noise. I hesitated, having had enough, then went back one more time. I felt I owed him that, though it would have been hard to say what for. He whispered, 'The wee guy was a madman. You should get the fuck away from here.'

Going back along the corridor, I wondered if it was possible to beat family feeling into somebody. That wasn't a nice thought; on the other hand, I'd never heard him be that human before – not, at least, since the early days when he was putting on the style to court my mother.

I went along past signs for X-ray and Physiotherapy and, under one for something called Oncology, realised I was being followed. Or thought I was. Or rather was sure and then not sure. A big slouching man in a crumpled blue suit and a shirt without a tie; he was so close the first time I looked round (without warning, because it had come into my mind I should check and with the thought it was done – 'a word and a blow', as the Irish guy said about his mother) I could see a sore inside his nostril where a hair had been pulled out. I convulsed into a walk and next time I looked back he was further off and that for some reason seemed even more suspicious. I wasn't going anywhere in particular now, but it did seem he was keeping in touch; near enough so that I didn't see me managing some clever way of shaking him off, even if I could have thought of one. Instead I stuck to the master plan. I went on walking.

After all, hospitals are big places; you could walk for days, allowing for exhaustion and the need to eat. Toilets, they've got those, and come to think of it counters where you could buy a pie or a scone and a cup of tea. Maybe after a couple of days when you passed the same nurse for the tenth time she might send for the police. Of course, it would be easier to spot weird stuff at night; if I kept walking until night, spot a stranger then, 'I see strangers!' and they'd have you. Have him. He was still there. I could hardly see for sweat. Fear-sweat cold on my back and the insides of my legs; you could keep your mind busy chattering in your head, but you couldn't fool your body.

By this time, I was moving so randomly I was on automatic pilot, and it crash-landed me halfway up a quiet stair. He came up after me, taking the steps three at a time. His fingers caught at my sleeve, and I leaped away from him by half a yard. That wouldn't work with the full grip on my arm that was coming next. Just then a door opened and a group of four in white coats came down from the landing above. I stopped and turned all in the one movement, the ballet of the terrified idiot, and at once I was in the middle of the group and going past him. They didn't squeeze to the side; it was their hospital after all.

'I wanted to ask you again about my mother,' I said to the one on my left.

His name was MacRae, we established on the way down, and if he was a doctor at all it was very lately. From something he said, though, I worked out what oncology meant and told him my mother had made a miraculous recovery, being superstitious for her sake. He thought I was a lunatic, or maybe that was the way everybody looked to him after a night without sleep. He couldn't work out how to get rid of me, and the other three were too tired to care or thought it was funny. I almost turned into the canteen with them, but I'd a feeling I'd worn out my welcome.

The short stretch between the canteen and the reception area was busy, and a public phone gave me an excuse to stay there. I bent my head to the dialling tone and spun numbers randomly. I listened to the squeal for unobtainable and looked wistfully at the exit. In the car park out there Mrs Morton was waiting for me. She'd taken it for granted I'd want to see how Alec was; and so it was her fault I was here at all.

The man in the blue suit interrupted my line of sight. He picked up the phone one along from me and put his tongue out at the side of his mouth to help him concentrate as he dialled. Being angry with Mrs Morton didn't mean I didn't want to protect her. Before he could open his mouth, I put my phone down and hurried off. He had no choice but to follow, hopefully before he could call for reinforcements.

I went into Reception and sat on one of the benches. He came and sat behind me. When I turned, he scowled at me. I had a feeling I'd turned a chore for him into something personal. He'd decided not to like me. Irritating him hadn't been a good idea.

After an hour or so, I began to feel exposed. The numbers on the benches were thinning out. Minute by minute, people were called and got up and went off. There were three receptionists, then two, then one of them disappeared into the back office behind the desk. I felt a hot breath on my neck and a voice like sandpaper on rust muttered, 'On your feet. If you fucking make me, I'll carry you out.'

I looked both ways. At the end of the bench, a woman sat with a little girl on her lap. Opposite, an old man was blowing his nose into his hankie and taking an interest in the result.

I turned and asked politely, 'What?'

'I need a shit,' he said, as if appealing to my better nature.

That's what his breath had reminded me of; another puzzle solved.

'If you're hungry, you'd be better with a sandwich.'

While he was thinking about that, I got up and went to the reception desk. The nurse didn't look up.

'Here, you,' I said.

She was putting a card into a box with a long row of them. I reached over and took it from her. When I turned it upside-down the cards poured out across the desk.

She must have had a button under there. Help came quickly.

Very impressive, but, of course, the *Evening Times* had run an article on how much security had been improved after the latest assault on a nurse.

CHAPTER SIXTEEN

S ecurity told me calling the police would be the usual routine. I told them I was getting over a nervous breakdown.

'At your age,' the older one said with a frown. Mental trouble in his book was obviously something they'd have called malingering when he was defending his country from the Hun; or maybe just lack of moral fibre, as my old headmaster would have put it.

The younger one was more sympathetic. 'You stopped your medication?' he asked. He had ginger hair and pop eyes and, ungratefully, I wondered if he was talking from personal experience.

At the end of the day, I hadn't stolen anything or hit anybody. Spilling record cards over a desk went more with having a screw loose than being a master criminal. And it was probably coming up to their tea break. They told me to push off. 'It's a kick up the arse you need,' the older one explained.

Left to myself, I'd have found an obscure side exit. Like all old city hospitals this place was built like a rabbit warren, and unless an army was looking for me they couldn't be watching all of them. Mutt and Jeff, however, insisted on seeing me out the front door.

Fortunately, there was no sign of the big man in the blue suit. Maybe he'd given up, or maybe he was wandering around the building looking for side exits. Maybe he couldn't wait any longer for his shit. To my shame I didn't check the car park. Mrs Morton, I told myself, must be long gone.

I walked for a long time, and came out of my daze near a bus stop with a familiar number on display. Not long afterwards, the right bus came along and I did what I'd done for most of my life. I got on and went, for want of a better word, home.

Going back there wasn't a bad plan. I thought about it as I watched the tenements turn into the familiar scabby houses of the scheme. Hairy Alec was in hospital. His girl might be grateful for word of how he was doing. Assuming she'd got over her opinion of me as a four-letter type, there might be a bed in it for the night. For sure, I didn't have anywhere else to go. Well, that wasn't quite true. I could have gone to a hotel; Mrs Morton had given me money. True, I'd stuck it in my pocket without looking, as if I could fool both of us into thinking I wasn't taking it. But it was notes, all right, a little bundle of them. Enough, surely, for a night's bed and breakfast. The truth was I'd no idea how much that would be. Thing was, I'd never been in a hotel. A boarding house would be cheaper, but I'd never been in one of those either. The heavies had checked out Hairy Alec's once. Wasn't there a saying about lightning never striking twice in the same place? I went home.

'What a fool you are,' Mrs Morton said.

That was later, of course. I had got off the bus and walked up past the waste ground and there at the top of the hill were a couple of kids standing looking at a car, a big shiny car which had no business being in the scheme. One of them had a stone in his hand and I could see he was planning to scratch a little revenge on an unfair world, so I suggested they fuck off.

The girl had given Mrs Morton a cup of tea. She sat there sipping it and the girl said to her, 'You were right,' and to me, 'I didn't think you'd be back.'

I made a modest salt-of-the-earth gesture to indicate how easy it was to misjudge people. All the time I was telling her how Alec was I could feel Mrs Morton's eyes on me. The funny thing was, I sensed that she knew how much I was leaving out.

We got down to that once we were in the car. I could see she wasn't happy, and I hadn't even mentioned the ragged scratch I'd seen on the passenger side as I was getting in.

'You were telling that girl the truth? Your stepfather's going to be all right?'

'Alec?' I didn't think of him as a step- or any other nearly sort of a father.

'Is he going to be all right?'

'He's not going to die. I thought you were going to wait for me at the hospital.'

'There didn't seem any point.' She cleared her throat. 'I thought if I talked to Bernard that might help.'

She'd driven home from the hospital. As she turned in to the road where she lived, two men came out of her gate. 'Just the look of them,' she said. 'They weren't men who'd any business being at our house.' She'd driven past without stopping.

'Was one of them a big man in a blue suit?'

When she said no, a big man in a brown suit, I told her about my encounter at the hospital.

'Bernard's gone mad,' she said. 'What are we going to do?'

'We could go to the police.'

As soon as I said it, it seemed like a pretty good suggestion. Let somebody else deal with this. It was way beyond me.

'Why should they believe us? Bernard wasn't there – he didn't do anything himself. And on the way to the hospital you said yourself your stepfather is the kind of man who gets into all kinds of trouble. Borrowing money,' she added, which made me laugh.

'What's so funny?' she asked.

'You make it sound as if that's the worst trouble you can think of.'

I say 'laugh', but I wasn't all that amused. It was only more hot air blasting out in contempt for her big house, her comfort, even the money she'd given me as a handout. Being frightened doesn't make people nicer to one another.

'What a fool you are,' she said.

After that we didn't speak, and I looked out of the window for a while until I realised we'd passed the Kelvin Hall twice.

CHAPTER SEVENTEEN

'Third time,' I said, breaking my silence.

'What?' she said, breaking hers, for which I was grateful. I'd thought she wasn't going to answer me. I hadn't anticipated the pleasure I felt when she did.

'We've gone past the Kelvin Hall three times.'

'Does it matter?'

'We're going round in circles.'

'I wonder what it would be like to do that for ever,' she said, so quietly she might have been talking to herself.

It sounded like hell to me.

'Not enough petrol,' I said.

'At the house, I sat trying to work out what I could say to Bernard that might make things right for you, so that you could get on with your life. And then you turned up with Norman.'

'Did you think of something?'

That might have come out tough. It didn't. I waited for her to find some magic wand of words that would wave it all away. Hope squeezed my stomach like a fist.

'After what happened to your stepfather,' she said, 'I realise how stupid that was.'

At a car park sign in a side street, she turned the wheel and went in. It was half empty, though it belonged to a large hotel that fronted the crowded pavements of Sauchiehall Street. I thought there would have been more cars, but she told me the hotel had gone downmarket and wasn't too fussy about the kind of guests it admitted.

'What do you mean?'

'Short-stay guests. Oh, couples for an afternoon.'

I supposed that was something she might have heard her husband discuss.

'If they're looking for us,' she said, 'it's better that the car's out of sight.'

'Is it all right to leave it here?' I wondered. 'Isn't this for guests?'

She chewed her lip. 'We could get a room. We need somewhere to think what to do.'

Whatever kind of hotel it was, I didn't think we could walk in and ask for a room without luggage – I'd seen enough movies to know that. She told me to open the boot and sure enough there were a couple of cases, a big one and a smaller. All I could think was that she must have packed them at her house, but I couldn't find words to ask her about it. I carried them in and stood back waiting while she went to the reception counter. All the time she spoke to him, the clerk tilted his head and looked past her at me from under his brows.

'He didn't think much of me,' I told her.

'Some of them think the sneer comes with the job,' she said. 'I should have asked for a suite.'

'What's a suite?'

She sighed as if I'd annoyed her, and said she was surprised they'd let me in the door even of this place dressed the way I was. As I was about to follow the guy who'd appeared from somewhere to carry the cases, she told me to wait for her. The two of them went into the lift and I watched the number above it change from 1 to 4. Avoiding the receptionist's eye, I wandered up and down until I couldn't stand it any longer and perched on a chair with my back to the desk.

Not long into an endless waiting time I convinced myself she wasn't going to come back; but she did and we went shopping. I protested all the way, asking why it should suddenly be all right to be out in the open among the crowds where anyone might see us, but she paid no attention. She led and I followed into Treron's and C&A and Saxone's.

'I thought you didn't have any money at all.'

'There was some in the house.'

'How much?' Alarmed, my first thought was that she shouldn't have taken anything. A strange thought, since it was her house, after all.

'Not a lot,' she said. 'A handful of notes on Bernard's dressing table. He might not even miss them.'

I got a pair of shoes that slipped on as if they had been made for me, and because when I took off my sandshoes there were holes in my socks she bought a pack of them as well. I got two Egyptian cotton shirts, put one on and carried the other in a bag, and trousers and a brown belt and two pullovers and a light-weight jacket with a hood to keep the rain off. And the funny thing was I felt as if everyone in the shoe shop was staring at us, but as I got clothes and put them on it got easier so that when we walked back into the hotel it felt natural to be walking beside her.

She led the way across the lobby past fat chairs, empty except for a couple having coffee, and pressed the button for a lift. When it came, we got in and before the doors could close a man stepped in to join us. He was a squat man, just up to my shoulder but he'd a thick neck and shoulders like a weightlifter. I was in such a state of nerves that I never took my eyes off that neck of his until he got out on the third floor. On the fourth, Mrs Morton, after a glance at the notice with room numbers and arrows pointing the way, set off to the left.

'Am I on this floor, too?' I asked when I caught up with her.

She put her key into a door. 'Come in,' she said.

Inside, I stood looking around. She closed the door behind me. It was a big room with a couch and chairs, and a dressing table with mirrors, and a bed.

'You're the one who wanted to save money,' she said. 'If we just want a place to take our breath, why pay for two rooms?'

'You shouldn't have bought me anything.' I pointed to the bags on the floor, among them the one stuffed with my old clothes. 'There wasn't any need.'

'Dressed the way you were, you'd have attracted attention in a place like this.' As if to placate me, she said, 'If I'd remembered the chequebook, I'd have used it.' When I didn't answer, she spoiled it. 'You do know what a chequebook is?'

I was upset, and it didn't help when the look on her face showed that she hadn't intended to insult me. She'd managed to do it without trying. It was true I didn't know anybody who used a chequebook. But I read, didn't I? I listened to the wireless. What kind of idiot did she think I was?

And then I thought of the room she'd been in at my house, a comfortless house in the middle of a giant scheme of identical houses, steel frames and pebble walls the colour of fresh excrement, slapped up by the planners on an empty moor that would have been better left to birds and bog water and the icy wind. What had she seen there to make her think I was anything more than an ignorant boy? Not books. Hairy Alec didn't go in for books, and he'd have got rid of any of mine the moment my foot was over the door. No, she'd seen shabby furniture and unwashed dishes, oh, and Hairy Alec's tart, unwashed as the dishes and half moronic.

Discouraged, I said nothing. I found a Bible in a drawer beside the bed, and when I looked round Mrs Morton had pulled a chair over beside the wireless on the dressing table. She switched it on and turned the knob past a man talking and a woman singing till she stopped at the kind of music that needs violins and a conductor wagging a stick. She asked, 'Do you mind?' and I shrugged. It wasn't up to me what she did, and anyway she'd put the music on so softly you could hardly hear it.

I took the Bible over with me and sat in a chair opposite her. Not the book I'd have chosen, but there was nothing else. I turned the pages and glanced at little bits here and there until I came to The Second Book of the Kings and got interested in this man called Elisha. He did a lot of stuff like watching his master Elijah going up to heaven in a chariot of fire and advising the king of Israel how to beat the Moabites, but what got me was that when a crowd of little children laughed at him and shouted, 'Go up, thou bald head; go up, thou bald head', he cursed them in the name of the Lord and a pair of she-bears came out of the woods and tore forty-two of the children apart. I thought it wasn't easy to know what to make of a man like that.

When I looked up Mrs Morton was lying back with her eyes closed. Whatever had been on the wireless, the music was over and a bunch of fruity-voiced pleased-with-themselves was discussing something or other. I bent over her to switch off, and she opened her eyes, making me step back in a kind of fright, and asked, 'Did you think I was sleeping?'

I went back and sat down.

After a while, I asked, 'Have you thought about what we should do?'

She shook her head as if at a novel idea. 'I was more resting than thinking.'

'We needed time to think, you said.'

'Yes.'

We'd found the time, and as a bonus the place too. We sat and looked at each other and then for a while we looked away. It wasn't that I wasn't thinking, more that none of it was worth putting into words, each thought like an old donkey going in circles round a pole. The donkeys plodded and every so often for no good reason ran in a panic as if under the lash. Not thinking, then; more like a three-year-old bawling, 'I want my Mammy!'

When Mrs Morton got up and lifted the phone beside the bed, I thought she'd decided to phone home. In my confusion, I didn't follow what she was saying. It was only when she looked over her shoulder and asked, 'Do you like steak?' that I understood she was ordering a meal.

A big room – there was plenty of space to bring in the trolley table. They called it room service, and it was terrific, like a picnic. I almost said so, but stopped myself in time. I didn't want her to think me a clown altogether. We had three courses and coffee. I don't think I'd ever eaten so much in one day in my entire life. We had wine, too, but it was the food I was drunk on and sitting in a room like this to eat it. She must have done all of that before, but the way she listened to me, nodding and even laughing, it almost seemed as if she might be drunk too.

At one point during the meal, I needed to pee but didn't want to break the spell – put it like that. Anyway, I didn't know where the lavatory was, and I sat there until I thought my bladder would burst and that was part of the strangeness, as if in addition to all the other things I was getting drunk on I was getting drunk on my body's poisons, too. Then Mrs Morton got up and without a word disappeared into the little entrance corridor. I followed her and stood staring at a closed door until I realised I'd found the bathroom. She came back, sat down, picked up her glass and smiled at me. I wondered how she'd feel if she knew I'd heard the sound she made pissing.

'We could have brandy with the coffee,' she said. 'Would you like that?' And when I hesitated at an offer so exotic, she pulled a long pad from her bag and waved it at me. The chequebook. One she'd been given to pay household expenses. 'Not that I've done that for a long time. But they're still good.'

Let her husband pay, then. He owed Alec that much. You couldn't go around putting people into hospital without paying for it. And Alec wouldn't mind us collecting on his behalf. Well, he'd mind like hell, actually, but for the moment that seemed only to add to the joke.

'Brandy would be great.'

When it came to it, I was too long for the single bed. She shook her head when she saw me curled in a cramped ball and made up a bed on the floor with blankets and pillows she found on the top shelf of the wardrobe. While I was trying to get comfortable wriggling into this nest on the carpet, she crouched down by the cases. She opened the big one, then pulled the smaller one nearer.

'Where did this come from?' she wondered.

'It was in the boot.'

She tugged at the clasps. 'It's locked.'

'I lifted it out with the other one.'

'It's not mine. I didn't bring it.'

'Sorry. I thought they belonged together.' It didn't seem worth fussing over.

She took a nightdress from the big case and went into the bathroom with it. When she came out, I pretended I was asleep, stealing one flickering image of her climbing into bed.

I lay awake after she put out the light. Something was nagging at me, something about the little case, something I should remember. It was like a forgotten word, almost on the tip of my tongue. Almost I had it.

Her voice startled me, whispering out of the dark. 'We'll have to decide. We can't stay in Glasgow, not after what happened to your stepfather.'

'I wish you'd stop calling him that,' I said.

81

CHAPTER EIGHTEEN

'Why *she*-bears?' she asked.

It had been like talking to myself, looking out of the window as the fields went by with never a word to show she'd heard me. I'd started to tell her about Elisha to give myself the illusion of company because I was tired of the silence. After a while I wondered if I was annoying her, decided I must be, but stubbornly kept on.

That morning we'd found the hotel parking area had filled up overnight and at first we hadn't been able to find the car. That's when the panic hit her. She'd walked up and down the rows, faster and faster. Following her, shivering in the morning wind, holding bags with the names of the expensive stores on the outside, I'd tried to make sense of her fright. She'd paid the bill for the room with a cheque. Was that it? When she'd torn a cheque from the book and handed it to the receptionist, the gesture had a touch of magic for me.

Afterwards, coming out of the hotel, I'd said to her, 'You could pay for anything with one of those, couldn't you?' 'What were you thinking of?' 'Like, food.' 'It got us dinner and breakfast.' 'Go round a grocer's with one of those. Anything you wanted, you'd just stick it in the basket. You wouldn't have to look at the prices.' And not just groceries. 'Shoes and clothes,' I'd said. 'Anything you wanted.' And then she'd said, 'Till the bills came in,' and become grimly silent.

Was it the idea of her husband having to pay the hotel that had suddenly frightened her? Then I realised that was shit. When we found the car and she dived inside as if I wasn't there, I understood, as if she'd spelled it out to me, what the panic was about. The two of us walking across the hotel lobby with people glancing as they went by, that couldn't have been easy for her. And then when we came out I'd spouted all that stuff about cheques. Listening to an excited, ignorant boy, no wonder she'd panicked when she couldn't find the car. Without the car, us being together made no sense. We needed the car to hide from reality.

And so for miles, looking out of the window at the fields, I'd told her what I remembered about the prophet Elisha.

It had taken me by surprise when she spoke.

'Why *she*-bears? Why not just bears? Why couldn't it just be bears that tear the children apart?'

I thought about it. 'Like in the song,' I said. 'Because the Bible tells me so?'

'Mothers would be less likely to attack like that,' she said. 'It's father bears that eat their children.'

'I don't think so. Are you sure you're not thinking of lions?'

'You don't really know. Don't pretend you do.'

'Lions,' I said.

'What?'

'Definitely. They'd eat the cubs if the mothers let them.'

She gave a contemptuous snort. Time passed and just as I thought she'd retreated again into silence, she broke out, 'Eve gets the blame for all of it. I always disliked that about the Bible, even when I was a girl.'

We were on our way north. I'd been disoriented and I'd been afraid and it seemed likely I would be again, but I liked the quiet throbbing sound the engine made, and I recognised the smells of soap and leather and perfume. Being in that car was like coming home, and I don't care how crazy that sounds.

I suppose you could say my life had changed since the day I drove away from the factory. I remembered the snooty receptionist and Mr Bernard and the fat man I'd thought was the bookkeeper until I met him again, and he turned out to be Mr Norman, one of the family. If we ever met again, maybe he'd recognise me. And I'd learned Mrs Morton's first name from him. Eileen. And Alice; I'd learned the name of a dead child; Mrs Morton's dead child. She'd been family, too.

'They don't look alike at all.' As soon as I'd spoken, I thought,

83

She won't know what I'm on about, out of the blue like that, why should she? But she did.

'Brothers often don't.'

'I suppose . . . Seeing him in the factory, I thought he was just the bookkeeper – something like that.'

'As far as I know, he handles the accounts. That makes him a kind of bookkeeper, I suppose.'

'He kept saying no one paid any attention to him. And he was Mr Bernard's brother!'

'Mr Bernard?'

I glanced at her in case she was making fun of me. She wasn't smiling.

'It's what everyone in the factory calls him.' Even his receptionist or secretary or whatever she was, I could have said; but I had a sudden picture of how she'd swung the tight package of her backside when leaving Bernard, and remembering that, I didn't.

'Did you see them together?'

Not Bernard and his secretary. The two brothers. I shook my head, and waited for her to explain.

She was driving fast, which surprised me, holding the wheel loosely and feeding it through her hands without any wasted movements.

After a while, she said, 'Don't make any mistake about those two. They're very close. You could say they're joined at the hip.'

There are people you feel you have to be talking to all the time in an attempt to fill up the silences. Somehow, now, it wasn't like that with her. We went along, both of us thinking our own thoughts, until I asked, 'Where are we going?'

Time for the simple questions.

'I don't know.'

That bothered me so much I realised I'd taken it for granted that she would have some idea of a place we might go. I felt one of us should have a plan.

'We can always stay in a hotel,' I said, 'like we did last night.'

'I can't use that chequebook again. Not unless we want Bernard to trace us,' she said.

84

'But that could take weeks,' I said. 'Isn't that right?' I meant that long before then surely all this would be over.

'It only occurred to me this morning,' she said, which didn't seem much of an answer.

I thought about that, until she said, 'Will he be all right? Your stepfather?'

'He'll live.'

'What happened to him was terrible. It might be dangerous, if you went back there.'

'I'm not going back.'

'I feel as if it's my fault.'

Funnily enough, I felt the same way, despite knowing it wasn't fair. What had she done wrong, apart from being in a car that I jumped into and drove away because I was being treated like shit? It was me that had been unreasonable. If you were young and poor, what did you expect but to be treated like shit? Like people said, 'You have to live in the real world,' as if there was another one waiting around for us to pick as an alternative. So what had she done wrong?

Be married to a bastard who just might be a crazy bastard? Well, yes. On that count, you could say she had to have some blame. I mean, she must have been there when the wedding was going on. She could have said, 'No, I've changed my mind, I've just realised Prince Charming here is a madman.'

'Are you sulking?' she asked after a while.

Not able to think of an answer, I scowled at her.

'I've been puzzling over why Norman was so interested in this car. What did it matter to him where it was? When I said it was in Howie's, he couldn't wait to get out of the door.'

But I was still working on my grudge. 'What age were you when you married him? Mr Bernard?'

There was a silence that went on until I was waiting for her to tell me to mind my own business.

'Older than you are now.'

'That leaves plenty of room,' I said.

She made a strange little noise between a gasp and a sigh. 'Now I think of it, tomorrow's our anniversary.'

'Hope he wasn't planning a party.' If he had been, the surprise would be on him.

Because she didn't answer, I had time to think what a funny guy I was. Another Max Bygraves, an English comic who'd been unexpectedly funny after he came back from the States. Tony and I had watched him on television. 'Give me a close-up,' he'd said. 'Closer, closer.' When it went to an X-ray of his skull, he said, 'That's what I call a close-up.'

'He used to,' she said.

It took me a moment to work out she was talking about anniversary parties. For something to say, I asked, 'Where does the road go?'

'Aberdeen, if we keep on.'

I hadn't ever been in Aberdeen, but I had an address for someone there. I'd memorised it from a postcard.

'My mother lives in Aberdeen,' I told her.

CHAPTER NINETEEN

I woke out of a dream in which I watched a woman's backside swaying like a pendulum. I was in Mr Bernard's seat behind the desk, which meant I had a good view. Almost at the door, the secretary looked over her shoulder and asked, 'You've a question for me?'

Opening my eyes, I wriggled upright in the car seat.

'You fell asleep on the way,' Mrs Morton said.

'We're in Aberdeen?'

After detours and walks, talks and brooding about all that had happened, it had taken us most of the day to decide that was where we would go. A decision not to be looked at too closely, made more out of dismay than hope.

I couldn't work out the light. Though grey drops of our breath covered the windows like a curtain, still it was too bright.

'What time is it?'

'Just after seven. In the morning.'

'We slept all night in the car on the street?'

I wiped the windscreen with the edge of my hand. A line of railing appeared in the arc of cleared glass, and beyond it grass and trees.

'Quiet enough here,' she said.

'Nowhere's that quiet.' I was a city boy. 'We're lucky we weren't robbed or killed.'

She got out and stood beside the open door, stretching and easing her head one way and the other. I shivered in a surge of cold morning air. 'What are you doing?'

'My neck's stiff.'

I got out reluctantly.

She was looking around in a kind of amazement. 'Aberdeen,' she said. Turning from me, she stared across to where opposite the park big semi-detached houses, looming solid and grey, were beginning to show the day's first lights. 'What in God's name am I doing in Aberdeen?'

She shook her head and walked away. I followed until she came to a stop by the gates into the park. Mist was being tugged like scarves off the tops of the trees. 'And your mother lives here,' she said. Under my fingers, the iron rods of the left-hand gate felt cold. There was no way I could tell if I was outside or inside the cage they made. 'Do you know how to get there?'

I asked one pedestrian and then another, and neither of them admitted ignorance and both sent us the wrong way. At last in a corner shop I got the right directions and found a street of weathered FOR SALE boards, windows with dirty, drooping curtains; and halfway along a sign which meant, if I had the correct number, my mother was living in a boarding house.

Only, as it turned out, she wasn't.

'Single room, bed and breakfast.' The woman opened the book that lay on the hall table and pointed to my mother's name as evidence for the prosecution. 'She left owing a week's rent.'

'When was this?' I asked.

'Would you be willing to settle the week? If she's your mother, like you say.'

'She was by herself?' On her own in a single room; whoever he had been, the new lover hadn't lasted long.

'Nine weeks she was here. The last one unpaid for. Made an excuse on the Saturday, and didn't come down for breakfast on the Sunday. When I went up, she was gone. Case and all.'

I went out and told Mrs Morton. As far as I was concerned that was it, but she went in by herself and five minutes later came out with an address.

'If she knows where my mother is, why hasn't she been chasing her for the rent?' I jerked my head at the house. 'Maybe she's lying about being owed money.'

'Who knows?' Mrs Morton said. 'Anyway, she settled for half.'

'You paid her?' I was indignant. 'What d'you do that for?' I decided rich people had no idea of the value of money.

'In exchange for your mother's new address.'

'How did you know she had it?'

'Town like this, it's a small world.'

She didn't know my mother. A woman like my mother might have left for London or Timbuktu. All the same, it had to have been worth asking. Stood to reason, I should have asked. I decided perhaps Mrs Morton wanted to find my mother more than I did, and spent the journey frowning over why that might be. Did she imagine my mother would take me off her hands?

I'd assumed she'd let me go in on my own. When I suggested it, though, she said, 'I'm cold, I'm hungry, and I need to use the lavatory.'

Walking up the flights of steps to the front door, I asked, 'Are you sure this is it?'

'You saw the name of the village. And this is the first house outside it. That's what I was told.'

I could hear she wasn't a hundred per cent certain. After the boarding house, neither of us had anticipated anything like this. When I pressed the bell, I heard it ringing but no sound of movement in the house.

When I thought about my mother, I remembered her in the morning, coughing, in her old purple dressing gown. Or sitting with her feet under her on the couch, picking a shred of ham from between her front teeth – she liked ham sandwiches, and I'd grill the bacon while she was cutting bread. Or making me laugh about something some fool of a man had said to her the night before. Even when I disapproved, if she set her mind to it she could make me laugh. When I gave in and did, she would join in and finish with a wide smile showing a strip of gum above big white teeth. That was how I'd always liked best to remember her.

When she suddenly appeared in the doorway, taking me by surprise, like that, even I could see she might be a woman men would want.

'What are you doing here?' she asked.

It wasn't an easy thing to explain. Inside, while I tried, she kept looking from me to the door through which Mrs Morton had gone to use the lavatory. Neither of us had sat down. We hadn't kissed or even touched.

'How did you find me?'

'Your landlady.'

'That old cow. Did you give her money?' My face gave me away. 'More fool you.'

When Mrs Morton came back, she said, 'What a lovely house.'

The thing is, she wasn't just making noises for the sake of something to say. From the street, we'd looked up to the house past two steep terraces filled with low bushes and heather. Here in the front room, with not a dressing gown or half-chewed sandwich in sight, a carpet in dark swirls of red and blue ran from the doorway to the bay windows. You could have put our living room in the scheme on that carpet and had enough space left over to tuck in our old kitchen as well. The furniture was big, solid, dark; the chairs and the long couch in blue leather. On one wall there was a painting of hills behind brown fields with a wee skelf of a pale moon above it all. On another, one of a harbour with old-time sailing ships. Both of them had an artist's name in the corner, made with strokes of a brush.

It *was* a fine house, and that amazed me.

'It belonged to Bobbie's parents,' my mother explained – to Mrs Morton, not to me. 'Bobbie keeps asking me if I'd like to change it. For something more modern, you know.' She looked round and made a little gesture like patting the air with her hand. 'But I tell him I know fine he loves it, and I don't mind one way or the other.'

Who the fuck was Bobbie?

After she left us, the Hairy Man and I lived in shit. Even when she was there, it hadn't been a whole lot better. If you don't have money, it takes an effort not to live that way. I can't describe how strange it was now to hear her doing the homes and gardens bit. Our gracious hostess.

Mrs Morton had that effect on her, and that must have been most of the problem. It hadn't occurred to me till that moment how odd it would seem to her, the two of us being together. I'd wasted all those hours driving through the night when I might have thought up something plausible.

90

When I explained that I was helping out because Mr Morton was my boss, my mother wasn't in a believing mood. 'You work for Mrs Morton's husband?' She thought about it. 'Where would that be? What does he do?'

'He has a factory.'

'You can't drive?' she asked Mrs Morton, who raised her eyebrows and said nothing.

'What's that got to do with it?' By that, if I meant anything, it must have been something like the rich don't have to drive themselves, even if they can.

My mother looked at me, then at Mrs Morton and then she got up and went to the window.

'Come here,' she said.

I joined her in studying the view. There was a nice display of roses in the neighbour's garden over the way. There wasn't anybody walking on the pavements. The only car in sight was the one we'd parked on the other side of the road opposite her gate. It was a quiet street.

'That car?' she wondered. 'He trusts *you* with that car?'

From that exact instant, what she wanted was us out of there. I wish I'd gone; it would have let us think better of each other. I got stubborn, though. If I'd been asked then, I'd have said because she was my mother and I felt she should help me. Now I'd put it down to having no idea what else to do.

As for Mrs Morton, I knew she must be tired, have a stiff neck, all the rest that must be wrong. But – you can't always tell from the way someone looks how they feel on the inside – she appeared relaxed sitting there. She looked good, as a matter of fact, and that, of course, didn't help.

My mother said, 'I have to go out now. I have an appointment.'

Mrs Morton stood up, too. They both waited. I didn't get up.

'Who with?' I asked.

'With Bobbie.' When she glanced at her watch, it shone gold. 'I'm already late.'

She went out and came back with her coat on. While she was gone, Mrs Morton didn't say anything and I kept my eyes stubbornly on the floor.

91

My mother held out an envelope. 'This came from your father. He's put his address on it. Here, take it. It's no use to me.'

It had 'Happy Birthday' on the front. I folded it and stuck it in my pocket. 'What does Bobbie do?' I asked.

She frowned, but couldn't resist saying, for Mrs Morton's benefit, 'He's a lawyer. A partner in the firm. His grandfather started it.'

'I'd like to meet him,' I said.

I got uncomfortable the minute she started to bite her lip; it was what she always did when she had a problem to work out. She stared down at me, chewing her lip, and then she turned and left without another word. It was only later, when the police arrived, that I understood how much she didn't want us there when Bobbie came home. I must have made her a little desperate.

'Are you hungry?' I asked Mrs Morton.

'You can't just make yourself at home,' she said.

She followed me along the corridor until I found the kitchen. There was a table you could sit a family round and a mile of surfaces and pots hung in a row on the wall. She watched while I got bread and sliced it and found cheese in the larder. 'Don't worry,' I told her. 'And put the kettle on.' I didn't see why I should do everything by myself.

You could say I was showing off.

She didn't object any more, but sat down opposite me and ate the sandwiches I made, some on cheese and one on a slice of cold meat I'd found between two plates. My mother hadn't turned into some kind of perfect housekeeper, which was a relief. Maybe they ate out a lot. Chewing, I looked out at the garden. It was big enough to have trees in it, and grass cut so short you could have stroked it with the back of your hand. I tried to picture my mother kneeling among the neat flowerbeds, but my imagination failed me.

'Why did you say you wanted to meet him, this Bobbie?' she asked.

'What?' I gulped my tea; she made weak tea. Though I was hungry, the sandwiches were dry in my mouth.

'Were you thinking maybe Bobbie didn't even know she had a son? That maybe your mother had forgotten to mention it to him? Was that the idea?'

'What idea?'

'A kind of blackmail. That she wouldn't want him to know how old she is?'

'Old enough to have a son like me?' The word 'blackmail' made me angry. 'I can see she wouldn't like that. *You* wouldn't like that,' I told her.

No sooner were the words out of my mouth than Alice came into my mind, the child Mrs Morton had lost.

She wet the tip of her middle finger and began to dab up crumbs from her plate. The sun shining in put a halo of light round her hair.

Without looking up, she said, 'It doesn't happen all at once. You have to stop respecting yourself. It gets taken away from you in bits.'

I knew she was telling me about sitting outside the factory in Morton's car. She didn't have to explain to me she was talking about that, I just knew. From the first, it had seemed so strange to me. Day after day; being so submissive to Morton. I still thought that was the most important thing about her.

Before I could think of anything to say, the bell rang and I was glad of the excuse to get up and answer it. I assumed it was my mother, come back because she'd decided it wasn't safe to leave me with her new belongings. There was a man on the step standing so close he was almost touching me when I opened the door. My first thought was it must be Bobbie, home early from doing whatever lawyers do; my second that Bobbie wouldn't have to ring the bell. Then I saw the man standing behind him on the path. The man on the step was small so that I looked over his head and the man on the path was so tall I had to look up at him. I knew him at once. A big, slouching man in a crumpled blue suit, he had pursued me through the Infirmary in Glasgow.

Before I could slam the door shut, the man on the step put his hand on my chest and pushed me back inside.

CHAPTER TWENTY

The small man had taken a seat before I recognised him. Mrs Morton was still at the kitchen table, looking bewildered. The big man in the blue suit had his arms folded, resting his weight against the wall near the door into the hall. The smaller man had taken a chair at the table without being asked, and as he jerked his thumb for me to sit down I placed him.

There had been three men in the group Mr Bernard had shown round his factory the afternoon my fledgling career came to a full stop. One was a narrow man with gold-rimmed glasses, the second a red-faced farmer type, and the third this little swaggering man with the build of a wrestler. His gaze went from Mrs Morton to me and then to the plates and the breadboard with the sliced loaf. He took his time and we waited and when he finished he looked back at me. He had small brown eyes, not soft, but hard like little polished stones, and when he spoke the words grumbled at the back of his mouth like pebbles rattling in a bag.

'Where's your mammy?'

'Gone out.' That came in a squeak. I cleared my throat and tried for something firmer. 'She'll be back in a minute.'

The threat didn't bother him. He turned from me. 'And you'll be Mrs Morton. I never had the pleasure. I know your husband well.' He scowled. 'You could say too fucking well.'

The swear word put me in a state of shock. I knew it, of course, and had used it since I was five in a primary school playground. My father had sworn, but not often and only when he and I were on our own. Respectable working-class women didn't swear, and decent men didn't swear in front of them. Even the Hairy Man hadn't sworn much in front of my mother.

The word was like a blow, but to my surprise Mrs Morton

didn't flinch under it. 'I don't know you,' she said. 'And even if you do know my husband, I'm sure you've never been to our house.'

'Why would that be?' She looked at him without answering. 'I mean, I could have been there when you were out, or up in your bed with a headache maybe – you look like the kind who'd have a headache. What makes you so sure I could never have been in your house?'

His voice was the same harsh grumble, and he didn't raise it. From the corner of my eye, though, I was conscious of an alteration in the stance of the big man in the blue suit, a kind of heightened alertness, an easing of his weight off the wall. It made me think, Oh, God, you've made him angry, and that made me angry with her. That's what fear does to you. I remembered my stepfather saying, 'The wee guy was a madman,' staring up at me from the hospital bed with his broken face.

'It's possible,' Mrs Morton said, and I found myself nodding, but then she spoiled it: 'But I don't think so.'

'Tell you this for nothing,' he said. 'I could buy and sell your fucking husband. That's why I'm here.' He gave a sneer that included me and the house around us. '*And* throw in whoever the boy's whore of a mother's got herself as a fancy man.'

'Oh, really!' On the exclamation of disgust, Mrs Morton stood up, but as she moved to leave the kitchen the man in the blue suit, still leaning against the wall, without looking at her or saying a word, put an arm across the doorway and barred her way. When she came back and sat down, her expression was different and she seemed smaller, as if she had only now understood how badly this might end.

'What do you want?' she asked.

'Either you know or your man's lied to me.'

'I don't know what you're talking about.' She glanced at me. 'Neither of us does.' She was trying to protect me.

He went on as if she hadn't spoken. 'If that poncey shite's lied to me, there's a problem. I might have to kill him.' He looked round at the big man. 'That not right?'

He smiled as if he was making a joke, but the big man stared back at him. It would have been nice to imagine he was waiting for the punch line. On the other hand, it might be he felt the answer was obvious.

The small man shook his head. 'I looked all over Glasgow for you two, sonny, and you've been here all the time, staying with your mammy. What room did she put you in?'

'How do you mean, room? We don't . . . What room? I mean, there isn't . . . There isn't a room.' The strange thing was that it wasn't fear for myself or Mrs Morton that made me babble. It was fear that in coming here I'd put my mother in danger from this terrifying little man.

'The one she put you in, either by yourself or' – he jerked a thumb at Mrs Morton – 'with her. Putting the two of you in the one bed wouldn't bother your mother, eh? From what I hear, she's an easy bitch.'

And with those words I knew, not who he was or why he had come here or his connection to Mr Bernard, but how he'd found us. I'd heard Alec Turner sneer about my mother too often not to know where that 'easy bitch' came from. I remembered him in the hospital whispering through his broken mouth that he'd tried to placate his tormentors by telling them he wasn't my father. Of course, after that he must have told them about my mother, everything he knew, including the last address he had for her. These two must have followed the same trail as us from the boarding house to here. What a fool I'd been.

Mrs Morton said, 'We haven't slept in this house at all, and we certainly haven't slept together here or anywhere.'

It was as if she hadn't been listening. I didn't think the little man was here as a messenger from Mr Bernard. Whatever he wanted, it was for himself. Why would he care whether we'd shared a bedroom?

'Where have you been, then?' He frowned at us. 'If you haven't been here, where the hell have you been the last two nights?'

Messenger or not, I hoped she wouldn't say one night in a car and the other in a hotel room; together and asleep.

She said the next worst thing. 'What business is that of yours?'

Instead of exploding, he turned to the man against the wall. 'What business is it of mine? What business is it of mine?' He started laughing, rattling the pebbles hard, the unfunniest sound in the world. 'What fucking business is it of mine? You're either smart or helluva stupid, sweetheart. Which is it?' What answer could she make to that? Certainly, sitting there too frightened to draw a full breath, I was no help to her. 'Oh, don't worry, it's my business, it's my own business I'm here on. Where's your stuff?'

Again I had no answer. The sudden change of direction left me baffled.

'Clothes, do you mean?' Mrs Morton asked. 'I brought some with me from the house. Does Bernard grudge me that? My own clothes?'

'They're in the car,' I said. 'We just got here. They're still in the car.'

He stood up and said to Mrs Morton, 'Let's go and have a look.'

'I didn't take anything but clothes,' she said indignantly. 'And . . . a little money.'

'Show me.' He pointed at me. 'Not you.' I sat down again. She picked up her handbag and the two of them went out. When I heard the front door close behind them, I stood up at once as if the sound had been a signal. 'I'm going, too,' I said. She had tried to protect me. I was ashamed of myself. I started for the door.

The big man said, 'Be a pleasure to give you a tanking, son.' He put out his hand and covered my chest with it. 'Just give me an excuse. See, when we were at the hospital I took a right scunner at you.'

'I just want to make sure she's all right.'

I didn't have the courage to step round him, and we stood like that till his eyes lost focus and he frowned to himself. To my surprise, he took his hand away.

'We can have a look out the front window,' he said.

As I followed him through the hall, the only thing I could think of was that he was curious about what was happening; or else he wanted to check that his boss hadn't driven away without him.

When we went into the front room, I went straight to the window from which my mother and I had looked out. Mrs Morton's car was still there, but two men in uniform were getting out of a police car, which had pulled up in front of it. Mrs Morton was straightening up from the boot. The lid was still down, so she must have been about to unlock it. Her companion stepped back as the two policemen came round the car to them.

I just had time to register all of this, when something that had to be a fist the size and density of a wooden club struck me on the side of the head.

CHAPTER TWENTY-ONE

'This is some car,' the constable who rode with us to the station had said.

The desk sergeant, though, was the genuine article of an enthusiast. He came out to the pavement to take a look at it. 'You could do well over eighty in that very comfortably. Not that I'd advise you to.'

'Because it's against the law,' I said, feeling better now we were out in the open air again.

'And we don't have the roads for it,' he said.

He showed no sign of moving. They'd contacted Morton in Glasgow and were – reluctantly, I felt – letting us go. Mrs Morton had already got in on the passenger side and I just wanted to climb in and get away from there.

'The lady's husband is expecting you back. And that's where you're going. Right?'

I nodded.

He studied me for what felt like a long time. He had thinning red hair and lashes so pale you could hardly see them. When he opened his mouth, I thought he was going to threaten me. 'The gentleman in question wanted you held till he got here. I explained to him that we had no reason to do that. He wasn't pleased. I asked him about those other two, as well.'

'What did he say?' I asked before I could stop myself.

'He had no idea who they might be, just like the lady and yourself. And I'm told they weren't questioned. They got into their car and drove away. They should have been questioned.'

To be fair to the two constables, the sergeant hadn't seen the size of the man in the blue suit. When I came to, alone on the living-room floor, I'd staggered outside, clutching my ear. The little wrestler had taken one look, clutched the sleeve of the big man as he crossed the road ahead of me and pulled him towards their car. In an instant they were off.

'At that point,' the sergeant said, 'Mr Morton hung up on me.' And he stopped again, as if he might say more but was thinking about it, blinking at me with those pale lashes. 'I was wondering if your mother would have any idea who those two were – not that I'll be asking her again.' I remembered that Bobbie was a lawyer. 'I was in the middle of a sentence when the man Morton put the phone down. I thought that was rude. Hard to tell what was going on.'

After a bit, I asked, 'All right if we get off now?'

I was round the car and halfway in, when he said, 'You're just a laddie, a silly one, maybe. You should be careful.'

I crashed the gears pulling away and watched him dwindle in the mirror. He stood watching us until we turned the first corner.

I tried to make a story of it for Mrs Morton. The way I told it, the big Heilanman doing the daddy bit, it might have struck a listener as funny.

Slumped down, she didn't seem as if anything would make her smile ever again. The afternoon had turned dark-skied. The ocean she was staring at, if she saw it at all, spread to the horizon cold and grey.

'Where are we going?' she asked, straightening up.

I hadn't thought about it. Back to Glasgow? The game was up. Presumably, Mr Bernard could protect his wife. I couldn't.

And suddenly I was angry with her again. It was as if I couldn't help myself.

'Tell you what, I've an idea,' I said. 'Let's go back and ask my mother what made her think the car was stolen.'

'Is that why she phoned the police?' she asked dully.

'What else was all that about?' I felt Mrs Morton could have told the police I might not look like much of a chauffeur, but who she got to drive her car wasn't any of their business. She could have told them something – anything – instead of sitting with her head down, lost in a dream. 'All right, forget my mother. Let's go back to Glasgow. After all, your husband's expecting us.'

A bad dream: mention of her husband had been the touch that turned her to ice.

When she told me to stop, I stamped on the brakes, jerking her forward, and pulled in at the side of the road.

Without a word, she got out, came round and opened my door. 'I'll drive,' she said.

'Do whatever you like.'

It's your fucking car, I thought.

Even on a main road there were quiet times. She spun the car across the road, misjudged and hit the opposite pavement, put it into reverse and then we were heading back the way we'd come.

'Where are you going?' I asked.

'What?'

'This won't take us to Glasgow. We have to go back.'

Wherever she thought we were going, she must have taken a wrong turning for we finished up at the harbour. We sat staring at the boats packed tight as herring in a box. When I wound down the window, you could smell fish and oil, with the tang of salt behind it. A group of men were standing close enough to touch the car, but when I tried to overhear, the language pouring out of them was strange to me – Norwegian or Gaelic, maybe, or just the way they spoke in Aberdeen, fast and guttural.

'What were they looking for?' I asked.

'He didn't say.'

'But he told you to open the boot?'

'And then the police came.'

I wound up the window and the men's voices faded.

'The only thing I can think of,' I said, 'is the small case.'

'The one we took into the hotel?' She frowned at me. 'The one I couldn't open?'

I nodded. 'I know where it came from. When we were sitting in the police station, it came back to me. Just before I came out of the factory and drove the car away, did your husband's secretary come out and put something in the boot?'

She stared at me. 'What are you talking about?'

'I was there when he told her to do it.'

'If the case is Bernard's, what interest could that awful little man have in it?' But then she went on at once; whatever you said about her, she wasn't stupid: 'Unless it really belongs to him?'

'And, for some reason, he gave it to' – I stumbled over the next bit, almost said 'Mr Bernard' – 'your husband.'

I told her what the sergeant had said about Mr Bernard Morton denying all knowledge of the men who'd pushed their way into my mother's house, and then I described how he'd shown the three men round the factory. Even then the one I thought of as the little gangster looked as if he came from a different world from the man in the gold-rimmed glasses and the red-faced farmer. She didn't say anything. I watched gulls swoop and curve above the boats.

'Don't you remember her coming out to the car?' I asked after a while, for the sake of something to say. 'That secretary, when she put the case in the boot?'

She looked at me blankly, and then with an odd defiance. 'Whenever she appeared, I ignored her. I tried to ignore all of them.'

Instead of saying something to show I understood, I sat in silence, staring at the gulls. Two of them squabbled at the edge of the pier, wings spread and beaks gaping. If I wound the window down, I wondered, would they sound like Aberdonians?

'If we're not going to my mother's, where are we going?'

'Not to Glasgow,' she said. 'Those two will be waiting for us on that road.'

That made an awful kind of sense.

'They can't be sure we'll go that way,' I said slowly.

'Where else is there for us to go? Isn't that what you thought?' And when I didn't answer, she added, 'That's how they'll see it, too.'

I wiped the cloud of my breath from the windscreen. Rubbing back and forward, I said, 'We could give them the case. If that's what they want, why not give it to them?'

'And then?'

I shrugged. 'Go back.'

'Back to Bernard?'

The silence went on for a time, and then she started the car.

We reversed out of there and retraced the way we'd come. What did she want me to say? That I was sorry for taking her from her husband? I was sorry.

I wasn't used to following routes and so I sat there waiting for the sea to appear again on our left and wondering what the two men would do if we offered them the case. Maybe we should stop and get it out of the boot so that it was ready to hand over. I had a vision of them walking towards the car like highway cops in a B-movie and me throwing it out of the window and us driving away so fast they'd never catch up. As I was thinking about that, we passed a signpost. It took a moment to register. It didn't say Glasgow. It said Inverness. I twisted my head round to make sure, but we were past it. I must have made some kind of noise in protest, for without looking at me Mrs Morton said, 'Maybe it's not about the case. Not for Bernard.'

What, then? I almost said that. The other possibility, though, was the obvious one. Driving off with a wife might be calculated to annoy most men.

'You think he's angry about the car?' I asked. That sense of humour will get you in trouble, the Hairy Man had often told me. However I'd got into this mess, some of it, it seemed to me at that point, had to be her fault.

She swung a look at me, sharp and hard. It felt to me full of anger or even contempt, but later I thought it might have been the first time I was not just a boy to her but someone she would take account of. After that the best thing was to keep quiet, and I did for a long time.

I didn't know anything about Inverness, except that it was in the north – 'Gateway to the Highlands', advertisements called it – and it had a loch with a monster in it. I read road signs pointing off to the right: Portsoy, Cullen, Portknockie, Findochty. Port this and Port that, the sea must be somewhere in that direction.

We came into Elgin and I spat out a joke I'd heard somewhere, maybe in a school playground. 'You know what they call a sheep tied to a lamppost in Elgin? A recreation centre.' It had been set somewhere else when I heard it, but to a city boy one small town is like another and jokes are adapted like that all the time.

'Don't tell me this isn't better,' I bawled at her, a smart guy talking to the deaf.

'What?'

'Seeing the countryside. Don't tell me it isn't better.' This time I said it in an ordinary voice.

'Better than what?'

'Better than sitting outside a factory all day.'

'You don't have to hate me,' she said. 'I'm not your mother.'

After that we didn't talk.

I don't know how often I heard her sigh before I glanced at her and saw how pale she was. The light was fading on the fields.

I said, 'We should look for somewhere to stop. I think you're tired.'

'This road seems endless.'

'If you want, I'll drive.'

But then the road gave us a glimpse of the sea and we were at the edge of another small town and she turned into a gravelled space in front of what looked like more than a large house. She booked two rooms and the landlord took us for a mother and son. He cooked for us, but I was so busy watching her I didn't pay much attention to the meal.

Afterwards, when I brought in the cases from the car, the landlord leaned out of the kitchen door and said, 'Your mother's gone upstairs. Is she well enough? She hardly touched her supper.'

'We did a bit too much travelling. She'll be fine in the morning.'

I told him we'd be going south the next day, towards Aberdeen. It was a stupid lie, but I'd begun to think like a fugitive and lies are what fugitives tell. At that, he told me we should take the coast road: Lossiemouth, Portgordon, Findochty, Portknockie, Cullen, Portsoy, Banff and Macduff. Lovely views, he said. They'd cheer my mother up.

There were two rooms on the left of the upstairs corridor. She was in the first one. When I knocked and took in the cases, she was lying fully clothed on the bed. What surprised me was that she hadn't taken her shoes off.

I dumped the big case on a stand by the wardrobe. She opened her eyes as I set the small case on a chair, and asked, 'What are you doing?'

'It's locked.' I pushed at the catches. They were square and looked like brass. The case itself was made of heavy leather and every corner was clasped with the same brass-coloured metal. 'If I had a knife,' I speculated. 'Maybe they'd lend us one downstairs.'

She sat up with a groan and swung her legs round so that she sat on the edge of the bed. 'What on earth do you think you're doing?'

I stared at her. It seemed so obvious to me. 'We need to know what's in it.'

'Why?' When I couldn't think of anything to say, she repeated herself, 'Why do we?'

'Because they're after us and we don't know why. Because we should know what's in it.' I pushed at the catches. Because I was curious. But how could I say that to her? Maybe that went with being young.

'Leave it alone,' she said sharply. 'It doesn't belong to you.'

Something in her tone made me blind with anger. 'Fine,' I said, and I stormed out.

I had just enough sense not to slam the door behind me, but I shut the one into my room with a bang. Before I could do more than take off my jersey, there was a knock at the door.

It was only the landlord. 'Your mother asleep?'

'I expect so.'

'Well, I was thinking, if she's still under the weather in the morning, come down and tell me. I'll make up a tray for her and you can take it up. She can have it in her bed.'

'She'll be all right, I'm sure she will, after a sleep.' I couldn't imagine what would happen to us if she was ill.

'Well, just in case. It would be a shame if her trip was spoiled. Weather's fine, you'll enjoy the run. See, if you have the time, take a wee detour to Portessie. They're quaint places those fishing villages. If your mother's all right in the morning, I'm sure she'd enjoy them. And it looks as if the weather's going to hold for a few days yet.'

He said goodnight and that he would see us both in the morning. I watched him to the end of the corridor, trying to make up my mind, then went and tapped at her door. There was no response. I thought she might be in bed or even asleep. Either way, she was all right, she wasn't ill. I told myself I was a fool and was turning away when I heard her calling from inside.

When I went in, her eyes were wide as if she might have just wakened, but she was still fully dressed though she was lying on the bed. She had a flush of red on each cheek.

'The man knocked my door. He says if you're not feeling well in the morning you can have your breakfast up here.'

'How nice of him,' she said. 'That's not usual.'

When she smiled I saw that she was pretty, and it occurred to me that that might be why the landlord was being so nice. I didn't know why I hadn't seen it before.

'I was being stupid about the case,' I said. 'I know it's not mine.'

'It's not mine, either,' she said. 'There could be anything in it. Correspondence he wouldn't want anyone else to see. Contracts, maybe.'

It was still on the chair. We both looked at it.

'Private stuff. I understand.'

She shook her head. 'No, not like that. Not because it isn't yours, or even mine. What I meant was that it would be safer not to look in it.'

'Safer?'

'Maybe that's not the right word.' She shook her head as if to disclaim it.

'I have to sleep,' she said, and her eyes closed, flickered open, not seeing me, and closed again.

I stood there for what seemed a long time and then went quietly out of the room.

BOOK THREE

August and Beate

CHAPTER TWENTY-TWO

When you are eighteen, appetite turns easily to hunger. My mother used to say, 'My belly thinks my throat's been cut.' That's how hungry I was.

'My belly thinks my throat's been cut,' I said.

She waited so long I thought she didn't understand and I was about to explain when she said, 'You're a growing boy,' and went back to staring out of the window at the fields going by.

Never mind me, I was worried about her. She'd come down though the landlord had offered her breakfast in bed, but she hadn't really eaten, just picked at the edges of an egg and pushed her plate away. He was concerned enough to come out to the front door and see us off. In the rear mirror, I watched him step out into the road and half raise an arm, as if trying to tell us we had set off in the wrong direction, heading north not south.

When we got to Inverness, she was asleep, sitting over against the door with her head resting on her hand, so that it seemed a shame to waken her. With a vague idea she'd feel better if she could sleep, like a fool I drove on.

The bother was I couldn't find anywhere to eat. Places I saw signposted might be only villages, or three houses at the end of a farm track, for all I knew. With every mile we were climbing higher, and now mountains that had a brown, sear look even in March were rising up high and stark ahead of us. At the sight of them the road felt suddenly narrower, not one that seemed likely to take us anywhere in particular. Just then, I saw an opening on the right and had the impression of a descending landscape with a suggestion of buildings tucked among gently rolling folds.

'What are you doing?' She'd come out of her trance.

'One road's as good as another,' I said.

She sighed. The minute she did, I understood how stupid and

depressing an answer it was. Fine, let her feel like that; we could starve to death, for all I cared.

Pretty soon I felt even stupider as the road turned into a single-lane one with passing places. The only thing was to give in and retrace the way we'd come. At the first likely-looking farm gate, I slammed to a halt and flew back in reverse. The car hit something, I braked and accelerated at the same time and everything went quiet as the engine stopped.

I got out. The back bumper was dented round a post of splintered wood.

While I was staring at it, Mrs Morton tooted the horn. Opposite, a board nailed off the straight to a post bore the word SNACKS in big, straggling letters as if a kid had got hold of a paintbrush. As an advertisement it wasn't much. If we hadn't stopped, I'd have missed it. There was an arrow pointing at the sky, which I took to mean go up the narrow road, almost hidden between high hedges, beside it.

I jumped back in and shot the car across the road. I didn't say a word or look at her. My silence defied her to say anything. She must have heard the crunch and felt it as we hit the post.

It was blind driving, a little twisting road, hedges giving glimpses of fields and hiding the way ahead.

'I can't stand much more of this,' Mrs Morton said.

She sounded alive again. Irritated but alive. I put my foot down, and then up again at once as the corner jumped at me. We were going about fifteen miles an hour.

This time the little faded notice was nailed to a tree: SNACKS FIRST LEFT.

Her sigh said louder than words how ridiculous all this was and I imagined another even narrower road round the corner, dwindling to a farm track and us stuck between hedges, not able to turn round. Reversing. I wasn't good at that. Hitting everything as we trundled backwards – rocks, trees, hedges, cows. I imagined Morton's face if ever he saw his car again.

But first left was a double gate into a yard with a van parked in the middle. It had a piece of what looked like cardboard taped on the end: SNACKS HERE. There was plenty of room and I turned into the yard and pulled in behind it.

'There we are,' I said. 'That was easy enough.'

When I got out, though, there was nobody in the van. Mrs Morton was sitting up very straight in the passenger seat watching me. There wasn't any sign of food behind the counter. Clean shelves. It didn't smell of cooking, it smelled of damp. There were buildings on either side with sagging doors, barns or byres, I supposed them to be. They looked neglected and probably empty. In front of me was a farmhouse, rough stone and peeling whitewash with windows set deep into the wall like old men's eyes. Rubble was piled at one end with a slash of red across it that might have been brick dust or the colour of the earth. A length of broken rone pipe was tipped against it. The place to my eye looked derelict.

Imagining Mrs Morton's sigh, I crossed the yard and knocked, then banged on the door with the edge of my hand as if chopping wood. I made an uproar, but only to delay going back to the car. I opened the car door and told her, 'There's no one there.'

'Yes, there is. A woman came to that window.' She pointed up at it.

I turned round. There were two windows above, and two below to the left of the door. Curtains hung, limp and unmoving. I wondered at the point of covering windows in such a remote place. A woman looking down from one of those blank windows and turning away: the image made me uneasy.

'I don't see anybody.'

She got out of the car.

As if at the summons of her knock, the door opened. I made out the shape of a woman, and then as I started to move forward the figure retreated. Mrs Morton went inside and the door closed behind her.

It was very quiet. As a city boy, I felt the quality of the silence. Then one by one little noises rose like shadows in water. Little fish noises of sucking and sighing; earth drying and old wood settling. The loudest came from over the fence, a stealthy trampling that stopped my breath until a plump brown bird bustled out from under a clump of bushes. Just as I was relaxing I heard the child sound.

It came from the nearest building: a wail, a gasp, mingled into one sound. It was unlike anything I'd heard before, but I knew at once what it was: a child distressed at being trapped in the barn, and I knew he'd been there so long that he was exhausted and giving up hope. Moved by the thought, I went and pulled the sagging door. Held by the ground, it resisted and then gave suddenly. As it jerked towards me, I had an image of the child crouching behind it, so that as I stepped inside I was looking down at the floor. Nothing there but dust and straw.

My first impression was of a couple embracing. Then the man stepped back, turning towards me, and I saw something hung behind him bound and struggling for its life. The barn was unlit, its dim air streaked with light from gaps in the walls.

'Yes?'

I saw that he was holding a knife.

'I heard a noise.'

'Not much of a one,' he said. 'It's tired. It's hung there for too long.'

The pig hung upside down. Blood from its throat was coming out with a sucking sound and dripping into a bucket on the floor. I wondered how long 'too long' was.

'I'm sorry. It was your notice. We saw it and turned in.'

'I heard you.'

'But I can see the van isn't in use.'

'What brought you up here? I can't think of a reason.'

'We saw your other notice.' And when he said nothing, I explained, 'The one on the road down below, by the farm gate.'

'You can still read it? I don't even see it's there any more.' He wiped the knife on a piece of rag. 'Nobody ever came.'

I wanted to be outside in the open air. There was a heavy, greasy smell which might have been the pig or its shit, and under that a sweet nastiness, which I got into my head was the smell of its blood. Muttering some kind of an apology, I backed towards the door.

Outside, I filled my lungs. I stared at the closed door behind which Mrs Morton had disappeared. I even went and peered into the car to check she hadn't come back, which was stupid since from where I was I could see perfectly well she wasn't there.

I didn't hear the door of the house opening but I heard it close. Beside me the man had come out of the barn and was watching Mrs Morton where she stood on the step with a tray in her hands. He'd moved quietly for such a big man, six foot, not much bigger than my height, but he'd have made two of me, beef to the heels and a neck to match. He had a round face that at first glance looked placid. The eyes, though, seemed somehow too large, bright and blue.

Mrs Morton called to him, 'Your wife said it would be all right if we ate outside. She said there's a nice place along by the stream.'

'You paid for the food.'

She answered as if it had been a question, though it hadn't been. 'Oh, yes, I paid for the sandwiches.'

'You can eat it wherever you want, then,' he said and went back inside.

Walking ahead of me on the path, she glanced back at the tray I was carrying and said, 'She made them on egg and honey. They're rather doorsteppy, the slices. And I'm not entirely sure her hands were clean.'

We followed the directions she'd been given. Going between the house and one of the barns took us to a path that went through a line of trees and along by a stream. At one point it was like sand under our feet, which seemed strange since we were nowhere near the sea. The stream was too wide to jump and the water ran quickly – even a fallen tree didn't slow it. The tree lay in the water and long strands of grass had woven themselves through its bare branches. The water had to make its way tight to the bank and slip past, but on the other side it ran as fast as ever, swirling round rocks and over lines of stones, each miniature waterfall filling the air with chimes. All I wanted was to eat, but she kept on until she found a place to sit on a bank above a pool.

'Mugs with lids,' she said. I thought she was complaining, which would have been a bit much considering I'd had the discomfort of carrying it all. 'They must have bought them specially,' and she smiled. I gave her one and opened the other. She took a sip and exchanged them. 'Yours has sugar.' The tea was strong and sweet. There were four pieces of bread. Two slices with the sliced egg between, cut into neat quarters; the other two coated in honey. All of it arranged on a plate. Mrs Morton took a bite, and then licked her fingers.

'The bread's cut too thick. But the honey's good. Local, maybe.'

'They might have their own hives.'

'I suppose. Honey from last summer.'

'Why last summer?'

She looked at me. 'Too early for flowers and pollen.'

I stopped myself asking what pollen had to do with it. In fact, I knew. Born and brought up in the city, though, it was easy to identify food with the label on the jar or tin and forget how it got there. Like the playground joke: it can't be easy squirting the milk into the bottle.

'You're right about the bread,' I said. It was hard talking with a great wad of it in my jaws. She had put her sandwich down again with only a tiny nibble out of one corner.

I thought of asking if she felt unwell still, but she spoke before I could organise the words. 'Perhaps she bakes it herself,' she said.

'I like shop bread. A pan loaf out of the Co.'

But she was busy with her own thoughts. 'Hidden away here, just the two of them. You'd have to get on well together.'

'There's nothing wrong with shop bread.'

'I don't think I said there was.' The angle of the sun threw leaf shadows that scattered like patterns on a carpet across the grass. There wasn't a breath of wind. The stream dropped like a twist of rope into the pool. The noise of the water and a bird singing somewhere only made it seem quieter. It should have been worth the walk. 'It's not something I have any opinion on.'

'You don't bake yours?' For a moment she'd looked relaxed, and I'd spoiled it but couldn't stop myself. But where did she get her bread? Where else but a fucking shop?

It was as if I'd forced her awake; only that wasn't it, she hadn't been in a dream, just letting her mind run on idly. A look of disgust contorted her face. She didn't like my tone. She didn't like being forced awake.

'A loaf from the Co,' she repeated. 'Two thick slices, eh? With chips. Or one of those flat sausages. Plenty of grease. A nice Sunday-morning *greasy* sandwich.'

I got up and started to take off my clothes.

From the minute I began, I didn't look at her and she didn't say anything, so I couldn't guess what she thought was going on, though as I folded my trousers and laid them tidily beside my shoes, socks tucked inside, it occurred to me she might have been expecting something like this all along. Wasn't that what women were usually kidnapped for?

I was down to my underpants when something else occurred to me. Sleeping rough. Toilet paper wasn't there when you needed it. White underpants.

I fled from her, down the bank at a run and jumped into the pool.

The sun was warm on my shoulders when I came up out of the icy coldness of the water. It was one of those days that sneak up on you and you realise summer's going to come round again, same as every other year. Four long pulls took me to where the last twigs of a drooping branch scratched the back of my head like fingers. I'd learned to swim in the baths at Maryhill, where the pool was heated; I'd never been in water as cold as this. Pride alone stopped me climbing out at once.

Swimming back across, I threw up my arms without warning and went under. It was deep and I went straight down, deeper than I'd expected so that I came up gasping for breath, but waved both hands in the air and let myself go down again like a stone. Same daft game as often when the class was taken to Maryhill baths, old Sammy yelling at us from the edge. Down until my toes sank into soft mud which wouldn't let go until I kicked up out of it, and overhead the water exploded and a dark cloud spun like a leaf down through its boiling whiteness towards me.

In the end it wouldn't have been easy to tell which of us rescued the other. I lay on my back watching the clouds go by and listened to her breathing until it slowed.

When she sat up, the wet dress stuck to her so that you could see the mound of flesh between her legs.

'You were under for a long time,' she said. 'I thought you weren't going to come up.'

The sun had gone behind clouds as we lay there, and as we walked back she began to shudder, though it wasn't all that cold. There wasn't anything to do but ask at the house if she could dry her clothes before we went on.

Inside, the house wasn't what I'd expected. For one thing it wasn't dark and for another it wasn't poverty-stricken. There was a pine table, the kind of table you might see in a picture of a farm kitchen in a magazine, and the whole room was like that, a place for cooking and eating and just sitting around. I thought at first there wasn't a wireless, but there was, tucked away on a small table beside one of two armchairs set facing each other on either side of the fireplace. It was true not much light came through the little windows, one at the front, one at the back behind the sink, but it was getting late anyway by this time and the woman had lit the lamps – oil lamps, she told me later – three of them, each with a tall, clear flame. And there was a fire, logs of wood smouldering in a grate. Mrs Morton was sitting at one side of it in a coat I suppose the woman had given her and with a blanket round her shoulders.

'You've had a fright,' the woman said to her. 'You should lie down and rest while your clothes are drying.'

That seemed to me a very bad idea. She could sleep in the car. All we'd asked was a chance to dry her clothes. Hang them in front of the fire, then; it couldn't take that long. Knickers and all – wouldn't bother me.

'Your clothes won't be dry until the morning,' the woman said.

They were flapping from a line I could see through the rear window.

'I have others,' Mrs Morton said, 'in my case. If you could give me somewhere to change.'

Her voice alarmed me. It was so faint you had to strain to hear it, even in that small room. I went and fetched the big case from the boot of the car. The woman led the way up a narrow length of stairs to where two doors faced each other across a tiny landing. I left the case in the room on the right, putting it just inside the door so that I had only a confused impression of a little room with a sloped roof and a skylight. Then I went down and waited while she took Mrs Morton upstairs. After a while, she came back and said, 'Your mother changed her mind. I made up a bed for her and she's lying down.'

'For how long?'

She looked at me. Maybe she'd expected me to sound like a worried son. Then she said, 'I don't think she's very well.'

The man didn't look any better pleased than I was when his wife told him we'd have to stay the night. He'd been coming in and out, bringing in logs for the fire, standing about, not saying anything. He actually shook his head at her, the lean woman, who was tall, too, though thin as a rail, but there was nothing he or I could do. The thing was, once Mrs Morton had agreed to lie down, she slept. Slept until it was taken for granted by the woman we'd no choice but to stay for the night. That decided, she fed me at the table with the man, a silent meal since he said nothing. She made eggs again and served them with slices of cold ham. The ham was amazing, thick and full of juice, but after what I'd seen in the barn I had no appetite for it.

When we were finished, the man got up and settled in his chair to read a book by the light of the lamp. When the woman sat opposite me and made her meal, I stayed at the table because I didn't know what else to do. It cost her so much effort when I tried to make some kind of conversation, I gave up and sat with my chin on my hand watching her eat. In the glow of the lamps, her face looked soft and round, and in fact she wasn't so old, thirty, I decided, or even in her late twenties, and he might be half a dozen years older. By the time she'd finished, light was fading from the little windows and I was wondering where I would sleep. I knew there were two rooms upstairs; Mrs Morton was in one, so I supposed the other must be the one they used; and, downstairs, there was only this room.

When she went out, I thought she might have gone to bed,

leaving me at the table. She came back, though, with blankets and a pillow gathered up in her arms, and made up a bed on a couch in the wall recess opposite the fire. All this time, the man read on, never raising his eyes from his book. Finished at the couch, the woman paused at the door to assure me my mother was sleeping comfortably. It seemed likely from her tone that she, too, was off to bed. When I was sure she wasn't going to come back, I took off my shirt and trousers and lay down. As soon as I did, even though I couldn't stretch right out, every muscle in my body sagged as if I'd collapsed at the end of a race. Yet I was tense, too, and lay with my eyes slit watching the shadow of the reader on the wall. Then I was falling, tumbling through the air with outspread arms, and started awake to see him turning off two of the lamps and go out carrying the third.

In the middle of the night I woke up soaked in sweat, and staying the night didn't seem just a bad idea, it seemed a terrible idea. Mrs Morton had bribed the landlady in Aberdeen to find out where my mother lived; last night we'd paid for the room in the boarding house; we'd used up coins to pay for the tea and the egg and honey sandwiches we'd snacked on by the pool. I had no idea how much money we had left and now we'd taken a night's lodgings without asking how much it would cost. I lay worrying about money and watching the last sullen glow of the fire until I couldn't stand it any longer. I found my clothes by touch and memory and pulled them on. In the lobby, the outside door opened at a touch.

It was hot and still in the yard, hotter outside than in, with clouds so low I reached up a hand as if to touch them. At the first step, I walked into a bucket that rapped against my shin, fell over and rolled away. I could just make out the shape of the car against the barn on the other side of the yard. It seemed a long time since I'd fetched in the big case.

The key turned in the lock and the boot lid swung up. The dim light of the interior lamp came on to show the small case. I knew we had to find out what was in it. In the bed-and-breakfast place the night before, I hadn't got up the nerve to defy Mrs Morton by opening it. Now, in the secret middle of the night, I didn't give myself time to think. I slid the screwdriver out of the tool kit, pushed it under the hasp of the left-hand lock and jerked it up. The same procedure at the other side and the two locks were sprung. I lifted the lid.

The case was full of money.

There was a flicker at the edge of my vision. I jerked my head round and saw a light in one of the upstairs windows. I slammed the boot lid down.

At once the light was gone, so quickly it would have been easy to believe it hadn't been there at all.

The little square lobby was dark, so lightless I had to feel my way along the wall until I came to the stairs. I went up softly, opened the door on the right, closed it behind me and stood listening. The skylight had no curtains and in the moonlight I could scarcely see the dim island of the bed. I made out the shape of one sleeper and then I thought there might be two and wondered if in the dark I had turned myself round and taken the wrong door. I held my breath and heard a sound so soft it might have been the sighing of my own blood in my ears. I crept quiet as an assassin to the side of the bed.

Mrs Morton was lying on her side. I bent close, and for a horrible second it seemed she had no face. Her face was buried in her hands; that was how she slept. She had shrugged off the blankets and her nightdress had come up to her waist. With a sigh she turned on to her back, and my nostrils caught the smell of sweat from her sickness mixed with the heavy warmth of her body's scent. Step by step, I retreated from the bed.

Trembling, I felt my way down the stairs again, expecting to hear a voice calling that only a thief would creep upstairs in the middle of the night.

When I finally got to sleep, I dreamed that I slipped my hand under the open lid, pushed it between the bundles and felt the money go all the way to the bottom of the case.

Between one moment and the next the windows were pallid with early-morning light. I lay awake, and it came into my head that I wasn't sure I had relocked the boot. I had to check, and saw myself crossing the farmyard towards the car. The image was so vivid, I thought I had done it, and started up suddenly as if wakening again out of sleep.

I sat on the edge of the bed for a while and then pulled on my trousers. The fire was out and the room with its thick stone walls was cold. I tiptoed over to look at the shelf of books beside the chair. In the dim light, it was hard to make out the titles. White and Morrison's *Geometry*, a blue binding, we'd used it at school; riffling through it, pages of propositions, each ending in 'QED'; dull reading it seemed. A thin volume in a dark wine red binding: *Adonis*, by Sir James Fraser. Palgrave's *Golden Treasury*.

I reached for the next book and remembered everything and knew the money was no dream.

As it had in the middle of the night, the front door opened at a touch. In this remote place, there was no need for locks. Who would murder us in our beds? I was smiling at my fears when I stepped out into the yard.

As I did, the man came into view, straightening up as if he might have been bent over the boot of the car.

'You're like me,' he said. He spoke softly, but it was so quiet each word was distinct. 'You have trouble sleeping.'

I was holding the keys and put my hand in my pocket to hide them.

CHAPTER TWENTY-THREE

He watched me as I crossed towards him. A bird whistled a few notes and fell quiet. It wasn't proper daylight yet. The dark was thinning, as if getting ready for the sun. Going to him was like walking into the shadow of a wall. I couldn't make out the detail of his face until I was close.

'No, I sleep all right.' I cleared my throat. 'I'm not used to the country – being so quiet.'

'I don't sleep much,' he said. 'But there are consolations.'

When he started to walk, I went with him. Without saying anything, he made it seem as if he expected it. He led the way along the side of the barn on the path Mrs Morton and I had taken the day before. 'I've seen the world get started every day of my life,' he said. He seemed a different man from the one who had been so silent and withdrawn the day before. The keys bit into my hand as I clenched my fist on them. As we went under the trees a wind coming out of nowhere stirred the branches above us. It was like a signal and with every step we took after that it seemed to get lighter, until by the time we stood by the pool it was morning.

He picked up a handful of small stones and started to throw them one at a time into the water. Ripples from the splashes wove a net across the surface.

'I missed your name yesterday,' he said.

I told him Harry, and was about to add Glass when he nodded and said, 'Harry Morton, right. My name's August.'

I thought it was a joke but fortunately didn't smile for he went on perfectly seriously, 'Like the month.'

I followed the flight of another stone.

'Up there,' he said. 'See?'

The bird was a speck hovering at the end of his finger.

'A sparrowhawk. Watch now.'

No sooner were the words out of his mouth than the hawk folded its wings and dropped. It came down on the opposite bank in a cloud of feathers, the bird it had struck in its swoop held in its claws. The hawk stood on its prey, looking around. The victim was bigger than the hawk that held it down, a fat brown bird with a white collar, fluttering its wings as the predator dug in its claws. With an effort, the hawk got a better grip and rose again into the air. As it did, the pigeon or whatever it was tore itself loose. I watched the two of them beat off in different directions. One to live another day, the other giving up on a kill and curving away in the opposite direction.

After calling it to my attention, he seemed to pay no heed to the drama playing out in front of us.

Another stone went into the water and he asked, 'What age are you?'

'Nineteen.' Nearly. Three weeks would take me to my birthday.

'And you've left school?'

'Yes!'

'As soon as you could. Hated every minute.'

I didn't much care for the way he said that.

'I liked French.'

'What's the French for hunchback?'

'No idea.'

'*Bossu.*' He shook his head. 'Just as well you gave up. You'd never get Higher French if you don't know the word for hunchback.'

'Right.' I looked for a smile; there wasn't the faintest trace.

'Schools matter,' he said. 'In Norway the Nazis took all the history books out of the schools. They wanted to have their own books instead. The teachers refused. It shows the power of ideas. Those teachers knew that ideas matter more than guns.' I more or less knew where I was with that. It had the sound of a sermon; the church service to end the school year; Bible Class, that kind of shite. But then he surprised me. 'We think in this country we won the war,' he said, 'that all our guns and armies defeated them. But there's no telling whose ideas will shape the world that's coming.'

'We won,' I said. 'We won all right.' I didn't have the courage to say to him he was talking rubbish. 'I saw the pictures of Berlin. In the newsreels, at the Roxy in Glasgow. Berlin was flattened. We flattened it.'

'Ruined cities . . .' He shrugged. 'We've had plenty of them before, from Troy to Warsaw.'

All I could think of to say was 'I never saw pictures of them.'

The last ripples from the stones were settling against the sides of the pond.

'This is a favourite place for us,' he said. 'When the weather's good, we often walk down here after supper. For swimming, sometimes. But it's deeper than you think, so you have to be careful.'

'Safe enough when there are two of you.' I suppressed a cartoon image of them ploughing solemnly back and forward.

'Like you and your mother. Lucky for her you were there.'

Realising he thought Mrs Morton had been rescued by me, I hesitated. But then, when I didn't say anything, he smiled and I wondered if he knew perfectly well what had happened. It was as if he'd set a trap and I'd fallen into it.

'My wife won't swim,' he said, 'because she can't be sure of being private. Not that anyone ever comes.'

For a moment, raw-boned and unsmiling they were naked in the cartoon.

'What happened to the teachers?' I asked.

'In Norway?'

'I just wondered.'

'They were shot.'

Of course. What else had I expected?

'If you want to carry on with your walk,' I said. I yawned, giving an impersonation of a man who wanted to get back to his bed. 'I'll maybe go back and try for another hour's sleep.'

The fake yawn set off the real thing. Great gaping reachings for breath stretched my jaws.

He shook his head. 'I don't think so. Young man like you, once you're up you should stay up. I'll walk back with you.'

He picked up a stone, small and white like the ones he'd thrown into the pool, bent to wash it, and then rubbed it dry between his palms. He held it out to me, white and pebble-sized. 'Souvenir.'

'How do you mean?'

'Keep it for luck. You could have died here.'

CHAPTER TWENTY-FOUR

When the woman said my mother was still unwell, my first reaction was disbelief.

'Go up and see her,' she said.

It was a tiny room. Apart from the narrow bed, there was space only for an old wardrobe and a chest of drawers, a chair piled with the clothes she'd been wearing and the big suitcase on the floor with its lid propped open against the wall. Seeing me look at it, she said, 'Take what you need. We're going to have to be here one more night.'

'What's wrong?' I couldn't manage anything better by way of sympathy.

'I can see two of you.' She frowned and narrowed her eyes as if trying to focus.

'We could go back to Inverness. Find somewhere better than this, somewhere you'd be comfortable.'

'I couldn't. I couldn't travel.'

'This is a miserable place to be ill.' The skylight was grimy with dirt on the inside and shaded on the outside with long, caked streaks of dried birdshit. The blue paint on the walls had faded to the colour of an old man's eyes. You could tell it had been put on over paper because a long ragged strip had come loose and hung down in the corner by the door. Incongruously, the clock that sat on the chest of drawers was made of marble with a statuette on top of a woman in a toga with naked breasts. 'It feels as if it's never been heated. Don't you feel the cold?'

She was sitting half up and her nightdress left her shoulders bare.

'I'm burning up,' she said. She rubbed her hand across her mouth. 'Could you get me something to drink?'

When I came back with the glass of water, she was lying with her arms by her sides breathing through her mouth. I could see her nipples under the nylon, and the curves of her breasts. She opened her eyes and held out a hand for the glass. When she sipped from it, water ran down her chin.

I didn't know what to do. 'Maybe if you ate, you'd feel better,' I said. 'Do you want me to bring you something?' Eating was my solution to feeling unwell. I knew nothing about illness.

'I'll lie down. Feel better if I sleep.'

When I went down, the man, August, had eaten and left already. The woman had put a bowl of porridge on the table. There was a jug of milk and I poured some into the porridge and added a lot of salt to make it palatable. At home we ate corn flakes. Even when my mother was with us, she'd never fancied porridge. I wondered if she made it now for her lawyer husband in Aberdeen. I sat spooning up porridge and staring into the bowl.

The woman spoke twice before I came to and realised she was asking me how my mother was.

'She lay down again. Maybe she'll feel better once she's had a sleep. If she does, we should go back to Inverness.' And I added diplomatically, 'We could find a doctor there, if she still feels ill.'

'My husband says you've not to think of moving her till she feels better. And not to worry about money, he says. We won't charge for putting you up, not when there's illness.'

I didn't feel grateful. I felt trapped.

I wanted to check if the car boot really was unlocked, but when I went out August was working in the yard. He glanced at me and went on piling up logs under the overhang of the nearest shed. After a minute, I made up my mind and went over and stood behind the car. Ignoring him, I found the right key and slid it into the lock. When I turned it there was a click and the boot wouldn't lift. All night, then, it had been unlocked. I took out the key, pulled at the handle to make sure the boot was locked now, and went back inside.

In the kitchen, the woman poured a glass of water and said I should take it up. 'She'll need to drink,' she said.

I didn't knock the door in case she was sleeping, but surprised myself by being glad to find her awake. When I showed her the glass, she edged up and made little gasping noises as she sipped the water. I wondered if I should offer to take the coat from the chair and put it back round her shoulders, but realised the little room was warm; the sun had come high enough to flood it with light.

'The woman says we can stay until you feel better.'

'When she was helping me into bed – it was just yesterday, wasn't it? We came here yesterday? She told me her name's Beate. That's right, isn't it? I didn't dream it?'

I shook my head. I couldn't remember being told a name.

'Maybe she was embarrassed. And she spelled it for me.' She spelled out the letters. 'A German name, I thought. Or Dutch.'

'His is as bad,' I said. 'August. Like the month, he said. Is that a German name?'

She gave a little shake of the head as if she was too tired to answer. And standing there with my head bent under the low ceiling, because I couldn't think of anything else I told her of our walk to the pool.

'The two of them swimming together,' she said.

'Just him. She doesn't want to in case someone sees her.'

I wondered if she had the same image of the two of them swimming naked under the trees.

'Hansel and Gretel,' she said.

'A kids' story,' I said, to let her know I'd heard of it.

'The two of them in that pool.'

'Deeper than it looked.' It didn't seem worth telling her again that he was the one who swam.

She went on, not talking to me, talking to herself, 'The pool under the trees in Gibbet Wood.'

It was possible the woman Beate had told her the name of the wood, or maybe it was a name out of another kids' fairy story that had come into her mind because she was unwell. Her cheeks were very red and when she lay back after handing me the glass her forehead was shiny with sweat. Even though I badly needed to, I knew it would be wrong to tell her about the money in the case while she was ill. Until we were away from this place, I had to keep it to myself. When I did tell her, what would she make of it? The strength of wanting to know that was unexpected, but then who else had I to ask?

'You should try to sleep,' I said.

I thought at first she hadn't heard, but after a while she said, 'Poor things,' which I suppose made a kind of sense.

CHAPTER TWENTY-FIVE

There came to be a kind of routine to the days, for Mrs Morton was ill for almost a week. The largest change in that time wasn't visible, but happened inside my mind, where from the fourth day I started to think of Mrs Morton by her first name. This came about through a kind of . . . I don't know what to call it. Jealousy? After two days of being confined to bed, she started to spend the afternoon downstairs in the kitchen, and when August and I came in for the evening meal on the fourth day it was to find the two women using first names. Before the meal was over, August, too, was on those terms with her, but I, who had known her longer and shaken her out of her old life, had to bite my tongue.

It would have been inappropriate to call my 'mother' Mrs Morton; and since I could not bring myself to call her 'Mother', even to keep up the pretence, I finished by having no way at all of addressing her. For compensation, from then on I thought of her as Eileen.

One morning when we were alone, I asked her, 'What do you and Beate find to talk about?'

'For one thing, South Africa. It turns out they aren't German or Dutch, they're South African. She was brought up on a farm out on the veldt.'

That seemed an enormous distance to travel, a world away. 'How on earth did they get here?'

Eileen shrugged. 'The war I suppose – it shook up everything like a kaleidoscope for so many people.'

'Did it do that for you? Was your husband in the army?'

She shook her head. 'No. Bernard's factory made things for the war. He was more useful there than in uniform. Maybe things would have been different if he'd gone to war.'

'Why?'

'I'm not sure I understand the why of it myself. I think a bit of him regretted not being a hero. I said as much to him once. I didn't mean any harm by it. No, more than that, I was trying to say in some muddled way that was how I saw him, as someone who could have been a hero. It was almost the first time I saw that special face of his – the one he made just for me, the one that said I was a fool. He used it more and more often and it took me to the end of my tether. Maybe having the baby was about ending that look. But it was no use. She died. There's no sense in things.'

There was a silence I didn't know how to fill. She blinked and stretched her jaws as if yawning out of a sleep. 'How did I get started on that? I've been talking too much. That's what happens when you aren't well. And Beate's a good listener.'

And where was I during these days they passed in talking together? Whenever I had the chance, I walked to get away from August's oppressive presence. The weather was unusually good: blue skies, often striped with white cloud, and the sun shone from early in the morning till dusk. The first two days I took the path through the woods to the pool. It wasn't a long way, but I didn't want to be far from the house and so I would stroll, stopping to look at the shapes the water made as it ran round rocks and over shallows.

At one point, a tree had come down across the stream and, caught in its branches, plants and grass like straggling hair had tangled into a barrier throwing back a pool of brown scum. The barrier wasn't complete, however, for near where I stood on the bank the stream jostled through a gap and even before it rounded the next curve had doubled in size, pushing out a space against the other bank. The second or third time I went by, I caught a splash out of the corner of my eye and then I saw the surface opposite was covered with circles. I decided there must be fish there in the darker water and that they were rising to eat, little flies, maybe, or insects too small for me to see from the bank. I don't know how long it took me to work that out, but when I started walking again I felt relaxed and pleased with myself.

QED, like one of the demonstrations in White and Morrison's *Geometry*.

The path, as far as I was concerned, ended just beyond the pool. Another fallen tree, held up by its broken stump, lay like a bridge across the track. Peeping under it, I was discouraged by a view of bushes. The nearest one had branches of small, tight-packed leaves and dark thorns long as fingers, which put me off the idea of trying to push through. And after all, what would be on the other side? More of the same – the countryside was like that. I went back and lay down to doze by the pool.

One of the afternoons I was doing that, I sensed a shadow and felt a little wind on my cheek. A cloud had slipped over the sun. The instant I opened my eyes, I knew I was being watched. Instead of sitting up, I raised my head very slowly: a red deer was drinking from the stream. It was the first wild animal I'd ever seen and I had the illusion that, though it stood on a patch of sand under the opposite bank, if I stretched out my hand I could touch it. In a moment, it looked up, flared its nostrils, and didn't so much bound as float to the top of the bank. Then it was gone.

No one was in sight among the shadows under the trees behind me.

Whatever they were like when they were alone, Eileen and Beate were quiet at the dinner table. Beate got up to serve, and when she put down our plates the four of us ate with our eyes on the food. August had that effect. Rebelling against it, I cast around for something to say and finally came up with 'This must seem very different from South Africa.'

'South Africa?' August raised his eyebrows and glanced at Beate. He smiled as if something amused him.

I looked at her, too. She stared back at me.

Eileen said, 'Beate's been telling me about the farm where she grew up, the farm on the veldt.'

'Did you enjoy it?' he wondered.

'Sorry?' Eileen looked puzzled.

'I expect you did. Beate tells a good story.'

'I see. Yes, I enjoyed listening to her.'

'If you like stories, I'll tell you a story. When I was a lot younger than your son,' he said, 'I'd regularly come home in the dark or first light. My father got pretty mad. He beat me for years and then I got too big. I knew he did it for my own good, and I didn't mind. But I got too big. All my family were like that, grew big and tall, the women as much as the men. I come from good stock, I tell you. Trekkers. When Piet Retief and Gert Maritz came up from the Cape Colony, our family was with them – 1838 that was. The Zulus killed Retief and Maritz. That's how our town got its name, Pietermaritzburg.'

'I don't think it was 1838,' Beate said. For some reason, she had become sullen.

'Wouldn't a good Boer know a thing like that? Believe me. In here is full of dates and facts.' He tapped a finger on his forehead. 'Don't try to tell me about South Africa. Anyway, I was a wild boy, but at a certain point of the night I'd turn my back on them all and head for home. Wasn't anything going on I wanted more than what I'd find at home.' He smiled, his gaze lingering on each of us. 'Going back, early in the morning, the streets would be quiet – as quiet as this.' He gestured at the night outside the little windows. 'Trees both sides at the edges of the pavements. But I walked in the middle of the road. You know why? Because it was a kaffir trick to hide among the leaves and drop down on you. A cart went round in the morning and you'd see dogs on it, a pile of them with their throats cut. Every house had its guard dogs.' Startlingly, he gulped at the air and swung his head from side to side. 'So you'd go along like this, keeping a sharp watch, and listening, and sniffing the air. Because you could smell them: they don't smell like white men.' He fixed his eyes on me. 'Maybe you are one of those people who don't like that said?'

The lamp on the shelf threw his shadow across the table. I didn't feel like arguing, but although I didn't look at her I could feel that Eileen was watching me. 'There was a teacher at school,' I said. 'He told us they didn't let Jews into his golf club. He told us they'd blown up a friend of his in a hotel in Jerusalem. I asked him, what about Germans? Did they get into his golf club?'

'He must have loved you,' he said.

132

CHAPTER TWENTY-SIX

My uneasy feeling was that, as Eileen began to get better, August didn't want to let me out of his sight. I tried to control my imagination and found a comforting explanation for the fact he had started finding jobs for us to do together. He'd been kind, I told myself, letting us stay and not taking any money. Maybe he regretted being so generous, and wanted something in return. When I thought about it that made sense. Let Eileen rest. I didn't mind hard work.

It wasn't all that hard, in fact. He gave me a scythe and taught me how to use it, and I spent the day after he'd talked about Pietermaritzburg cutting overgrown grass and clearing stones off a patch of ground at the side of the house until I could smell my own sweat. The day after, I helped him to rehang a gate in a fence which made a narrow yard in front of the pen where he kept three pigs. As we worked, one of them lay on her side, watching with small, intent eyes, while a line of young fastened themselves on the teats along her belly.

We planted potatoes, too, digging the furrows and dropping them in about a foot apart and then pulling the soil across the rows. That was done on another bit of ground, between the end of the house and where the line of trees began. It was a fair size, but more like an oversized plot in a garden than what I would have thought of as a field. On the other side of the barn and sheds, there was a pasture, still not all that big, in which a solitary cow, brown and shaggy with curved horns, grazed forlornly.

The strange thing is that I slept well. Hard work in the open air meant there were no bad dreams. It disturbed me, though, how little he spoke when we were alone. Even when we had a break at midday, for a thick ham sandwich and a glass of milk, he chewed with his head over a book. While we worked, if I looked up and found his eye on me, it was only for an instant, then he glanced away. His instructions were clear and he seemed content with how I followed them. All the time, I was aware of the raw power of him, the wads of muscle at the sides of his neck, the hands like shovels; yet to admit to finding that menacing would have been shameful, or so it seemed to me.

I disliked the scythe in those big hands and was glad when, after a few long, slow sweeps to show me how, he passed it over to me. 'It's sharp,' he said. 'Mind you don't cut off your feet.'

The day after we put in the potatoes I overslept and opened my eyes to see Beate wiping dishes and stacking them at the side of the sink. I slipped out of the couch bed while she had her back to me; but she turned while I was balanced on one leg to get into my trousers.

'Is it all right if I take a piece of bread?' I asked, turning away from her to pull up the zip.

'No, it isn't,' she said. 'What kind of breakfast would that be? I'll make you porridge.'

I sat at the table and watched as she put a handful of meal in a pot with water. She stirred the pot on the stove and I looked at the length of her back and her legs under the dress. The dress was grey and that was the impression she'd made on me, quiet and grey. The material of it was thin, however, and when she bent the cloth settled round her hips so that I could see the shape of her bottom under it. After all, she wasn't that much older than me, a handful of years, not more than ten, surely? Even her face, which had seemed so dull before, had a kind of sparkle when she turned unexpectedly from the stove and caught my eye on her.

'How much do you want in the bowl? My husband takes it full.'

'Plenty of room for the milk would be fine, thanks.'

When she put the bowl in front of me, I expected her to get on with her work. Instead, she sat down across the table and watched me as I ate, the first spoonful the cream of the milk and then the porridge itself with an aftertaste of salt.

'Where does August want me this morning?' I asked.

'He's not here. Did he not say yesterday?'

I shook my head. 'No.'

'He's away to town for some shopping.'

'Oh.'

'So you can take it easy.'

'I don't mind working.'

'It's done you good. You're not so pale as you were.'

I didn't know what to say to that. She studied me while I ate. Embarrassed, I said, 'I'll take some breakfast up.'

'For your mother? But she's away, too.'

'Where?' I was on the point of starting up and running out to see if the car was gone.

'She was down by the time he was getting ready, and he asked if she wanted to go with him.'

'And she just went?' I heard the break in my voice and cleared my throat.

She looked at me. Her eyes were the same green as the eyes of a redheaded girl who'd sat across the aisle in the French class in my last year at school; the special hard, flat green that goes with red hair, though Beate's was brown. Until that morning when we were alone, it was as if I hadn't really seen her at all.

It was into the afternoon before they came back. I watched as August took a box out of the back seat and carried it into the house.

Eileen smiled at me as she got out of the car. 'I've been well looked after. I spent most of the time sitting on a bench in the sun while August shopped. And then we went to a little café and had lunch.' I stared at her without replying. I wondered if he'd found his tongue with her. 'I enjoyed myself,' she said.

'I didn't know you'd gone.' I couldn't help making it sound like an accusation.

'You slept all through us leaving. He must have tired you out yesterday.'

For no good reason, this offended me. I scowled at her, but she didn't seem to notice.

'I don't feel sick.' She stretched her arms wide. 'It's wonderful to feel human again.'

When we went inside, the box of shopping was sitting on the kitchen table. To help Beate, who was putting away the contents, I began to hand her packets of salt, blocks of soap, toilet paper, a floppy package in a wrapping of thick white paper that might have held fish; and, surprising me, half a dozen tins of custard.

Seeing me look at them, Beate said, 'That's August's treat.'

I didn't know whether to smile or nod. Maybe he ate them all himself, and she was warning me off.

Anyway, treat or not, none of the tins appeared at that evening's meal. While we ate – the usual solid plateful of meat and potatoes – Eileen tried to make sociable conversation. It was an uphill battle, for August had fallen back on silence, making me wonder if it was my company which had that effect on him. It was a relief when, unexpectedly, Beate began to talk about her life as a child on a farm far out on the South African veldt.

'We were surrounded by space to the horizons,' she said. 'A wonderful life for a child, like being on an island. And the sky at night was crammed with stars.'

'Plenty of stars here,' August said. It was the first time he'd spoken during the meal. If he'd found his tongue when he was alone with Eileen, he seemed to have lost it again.

'They aren't the same stars,' she said on an odd note of triumph. 'I used to lie on my back and look up at them. It felt like falling.'

'Were you an only child?' Eileen asked.

'I was a lonely one. Lonely all the time. Until I met August.'

Putting a forkful of food in his mouth, he glanced up at her but said nothing.

'Did you meet as children?' Eileen sounded startled, but somehow pleased. Maybe she thought that would have been romantic.

'Oh, no!' She shook her head vigorously. It was very emphatic. *She* doesn't think it's romantic, I thought sourly.

'Beate came to town to work as a servant.' August broke his silence again. Wiping his mouth, he said, 'It happened to be in my father's house.'

'Not polishing and dusting,' Beate said. She frowned at him, lines wrinkling her high, pale forehead. 'Blacks did that kind of work.'

'We could do with one here,' he said. 'A strong kaffir girl.'

'We had plenty of kaffirs on the farm,' she said, 'men and women. My mother kept the women in the house busy, and my father worked the men hard – he had no patience with slackers.'

'You can't stop a kaffir taking it easy,' August said. 'It's their nature. If it wasn't for the white man they'd sit on their' – he glanced at Eileen – 'sit around all day. Nothing was done with the land when they had it.'

Eileen looked from husband to wife, then at me. I chewed and stared down at my plate. There didn't seem much room for either of us to say anything. Probing, as if with sword-tips testing for weakness, our hosts were absorbed with each other.

'When I was eleven I saw my father beat a kaffir to death,' Beate said. 'He thrashed him with a long black whip that was used on the cattle.'

I realised my mouth had fallen open, and shut it.

'They call a whip like that a sjambok.' August offered this matter-of-factly, a piece of information we might find of interest. It didn't help.

To my amazement, Eileen asked, 'Is that how you pronounce it?'

August lifted his black eyebrows at her and nodded.

I couldn't believe she'd heard what Beate had just said.

'That's the correct way,' he said as if settling an argument.

'The whip took strips of flesh off,' Beate intervened firmly. 'Blood came up in sprays, I've never forgotten that. It was all so amazing. I couldn't look away. When my father finished, you could see the old man's spine: white bone and tatters of black skin.'

'What happened to him?' I asked. I was surprised to hear my voice, thin and almost trembling.

'They took him to hospital, but he died a week later.'

'Your father, I mean.' Your fucking brute of a father. 'At his trial.'

'Trial?' August wondered. 'I don't think so.'

'How could he get away with that?'

'Oh, but he didn't,' Beate said. She was answering me, but she didn't take her eyes from August. 'He *was* taken to court. I remember how angry he was about being fined. So, you see, he didn't get away with it.'

Head to one side, Eileen was gazing at Beate and I couldn't catch her eye.

'Terrible things happen in the world,' August said.

'Like the Nazis,' his wife said.

'Why bring them up?' he asked with a frown.

I knew the kind of terrible thing Beate was thinking of.

'Like the teachers in Norway,' I said.

Husband and wife turned on me identical expressions of surprise. It was as if they had forgotten I was there.

He got up abruptly. 'I'm going to bed.'

'Good night,' Eileen said, but he was already out of the room.

When Beate yawned, she didn't cover her mouth with her hand. Before it closed, she wiped her tongue over her lips. Quick and pink, it was like a small animal.

'If it's that time,' she said.

In a moment, Eileen and I were left on our own.

'What was that about?' I wondered if she had heard me. My voice wasn't much above a whisper. I needed her to say something reassuring.

'They wanted to get to bed,' she said.

'It's not late.' I waited. Then I said, 'I meant all that stuff about her father. Beating an old man to death with a whip.'

'A sjambok.'

'That's not how he said it.'

'Maybe it's a word he's only read.'

'That doesn't make any sense.' Not with him being South African, I meant.

'I suppose not.'

The way she said it shut me out of whatever she might be thinking.

'Why would she tell us a thing like that?' I asked.

'How should I know what it was about, any more than you?'

138

CHAPTER TWENTY-SEVEN

I woke in the morning out of a strange dream. By the time I opened my eyes it was gone, leaving only the image of a clock with a statuette of a woman on top. She was half undraped, so that her little breasts were uncovered. Mired in sleep still, I felt them under my fingers, cold and hard as pebbles. As I lay thinking about them, I remembered that it was the clock in Eileen's room upstairs. I'd seen it that first day when I took up her case, out of place in that bare room beside the narrow bed.

I'd pulled the blanket up over my head as I slept. Going by the other mornings, I assumed August was already out and about, but lying there I missed the smell of food and the sounds Beate made as she moved about. When I tugged the blanket off, the room was empty. According to the clock on the wall, it was just after seven. Half dressed, still pulling on my shirt, I went to the window and there husband and wife were in the middle of the yard, heads bowed as if staring at the ground, silent but close together. I took a step back, not wanting to be seen, but as I did she reached out her hand and he took it, and hand in hand the two of them went out of the yard towards the woods. The air was full of early sunlight. Black shadows from the byre and the shed beside it stretched half across the yard. If I was surprised to see them go off like that, it was because I'd a vague idea that for people on farms the country was for work not pleasure. All the same, if they wanted to go walking, what business was it of mine? It was a fine morning.

I decided Eileen must still be asleep; most mornings she'd been sleeping, or at least not coming down, until after eight. I cut a slice from the loaf Beate had made the day before and found butter in a clay dish on a shelf. No cheese, though – maybe I was looking in the wrong place – and I didn't want to risk trying to make porridge. I didn't even fill a kettle to boil water on the range for tea. Instead, I poured milk into a cup and was making a glum, cold breakfast at the table when Eileen appeared.

'You're early,' I told her. It wasn't much of a greeting, but I was feeling sorry for myself.

'I'm a lot better. Not entirely well, but able to travel.' She lowered her voice, as if not wanting to be overheard. 'I think we should leave this morning. I'll say so to Beate.'

'Beate isn't here.' She looked at me in surprise. 'The two of them have gone off for a walk.' I smiled, thinking she would find it as odd as I had.

After a moment, she went to the window and looked out. 'Where to?'

'Towards the woods. It's nice out. They went off hand in hand.'

'They didn't say where they were going? Or how long they'd be?'

'I didn't speak to them.'

She stood looking at me, biting her lip in silence.

'Can you make porridge?' I asked.

'What?'

I didn't think it was such a stupid question. For God's sake, it was breakfast time.

'Or tea? If you'll make tea, I'll have a proper look and see if I can find something to eat. Eggs or something.'

'I packed my case last night,' she said. 'Go and bring it down.'

Though she spoke quietly, I got up at once and didn't walk but ran up the stairs. It was as if with the first movement my body remembered what I had suppressed: how uneasy I felt about the man of the house. Going in, I thought it would be the last time I saw that room. The skylight window was pushed up, held open by a thin metal bar. In the space between the window and the frame, a spider had hung the loose weave of its net. The clock chimed eight as I lifted the case from where it lay beside the bed. The little statuette bowed its head to avoid my glance. I had dreamed of it as more brazen.

Going back down, the case bumped awkwardly against the wall of the narrow staircase.

'Now?' I asked.

'Why not? We've nothing to stay for.'

'They'll think it's funny if we just go. Shouldn't we thank them?'

'Can we just go, please?'

Only perversity had made me argue. Of course I wanted to get out of there. Maybe I was trying to impress her, safe in the knowledge that she was determined to leave. I put on my jacket and automatically felt to make sure the handful of coins was still in the side pocket.

Since that first night, I hadn't tried to check the boot, afraid perhaps of finding it empty. Relief flooded through me when I saw the small case was still there. Going back into the world, it seemed that after all we would have money, unless it had all been a middle-of-the-night dream. Pushing it to the back of the boot, I laid the big case in front of it like a barrier. Time enough once we were well on our way to share the discovery with Eileen.

The yard was hot and still. I stood with the boot lid in my hand, feeling vulnerable. When Eileen appeared, I slammed it shut, alarming myself with the noise.

'I decided it might be better if we left a note,' she explained, as if apologising.

Her eyes were tired. I realised suddenly how much thinner she was.

'I'll drive if you want,' I said. 'You could rest.'

She thought about it, then shook her head. 'If it gets too much for me, we can change places.'

I'd no argument with that. I'd no argument with anything. We were leaving!

I got in on the passenger side. As Eileen was sliding behind the wheel, I said, 'If those two come back, don't stop. Just keep going.'

She closed the door. We sat together, side by side again. I had an extraordinary feeling of peace and security. It was as if I had come home.

When she turned the key, it made a clicking sound. She glanced at me and tried again. The engine didn't roar into life. As she tried for the third time, there came the same dry click.

I looked down as I felt Eileen's hand grip my wrist. Before I could ask what was wrong, I saw for myself. In the shadow where the path emerged from the woods, a man and woman stood. They seemed to be holding hands and there was no way of telling how long they'd been there.

CHAPTER TWENTY-EIGHT

We were waiting for August to come back.

There hadn't been any fuss when they came out from under the trees and crossed to the car. He'd put up the bonnet and fiddled around and asked Eileen to start the engine again. When it wouldn't, I got out and stood beside Beate watching him. I recognised the engine mounting and the rod for testing oil and the place where you put water in and the other place where you put liquid in for the windscreen wash. That was about it. Then August went and came back with a box of spanners and Beate asked about a wire hanging loose that I hadn't even noticed. He frowned at her, and went to work without answering. After he'd taken the starting motor out, it didn't matter what the wire might have been, so I didn't ask.

He'd gone into town, taking the motor with him, and the three of us were in the kitchen, waiting for him to come back. Beate was doing a washing at the sink by the back window. Eileen and I were sitting at the table.

I leaned forward and said to her quietly, 'Come for a walk.'

Beate turned and frowned at me. 'Leave your mother alone,' she said. 'She's tired.'

'We don't have to go far.'

Eileen shook her head.

I was desperate for her to come. I needed to tell her about the money. As well, I wanted to tell her about that loose wire; wanted her to say it was nothing; that I was imagining things.

'August won't be long,' Beate said.

'We should be here when he gets back,' Eileen said.

She was gentle and reasonable and immovable. She kept repeating how good it was of August to take the motor to his friend – 'A friend,' he'd said, shrugging, when Eileen explained we might not have enough money.

Beate wiped her hands on a towel, leaned back against the sink and didn't even pretend not to be listening. In the end, I scowled at both of them and went out.

I didn't take the path to the pool. Needing to be free of the place, I went out on to the road and turned left, away from the junction with the sign that had directed us here. I assumed that the junction would be on the way to the nearest town with a garage. The last thing I wanted was to meet August returning.

In the dimly lit kitchen, enclosed by its thick stone walls, I hadn't realised how hot the day had turned. In half a mile, my shirt was sticking to my back. Mountains folded one behind the other in the distance. Fields, dipping and rising, spread on both sides of the narrow road. Trees lined against the sky on top of a rise, all leaning the same way. Gradually the landscape and silence imposed an unexpected peace. I had no names for the mountains. I didn't know one tree from another. I knew nothing about farm beasts or about birds or the wild things in the grass. I had no idea of how people lived in such places, what was natural, what men had made, what any of it meant. I had only impressions: big curves of blue or green as if slashed on to a painting from a loaded brush. The wonderful thing was to be alone, no one looking at me, the world mine. I spun slowly till the empty world tilted about me.

As the world wound down, from out of nowhere came the uproar of a big American voice, accompanied by a band – drums thumping, trumpets blaring – bawling from full lungs: 'If ever the devil was born without a pair of horns, it was you, Jezebel, it was you. If ever an angel fell, Jezebel, it was you, Jezebel, it was you. If ever a pair of eyes promised paradise, deceiving me, grieving me, leavin' me blue, Jezebel . . .'

Round a turn in the road, I came on a man at the edge of the field, crouched over a sheep on its back with its legs waving in the air. At the instant I stopped to watch, with a heave he threw it on to its feet. It exploded out of his grip and bolted off, and he straightened up and studied me.

'If ever the devil's plan was made to torment man, it was you, Jezebel, it . . .'

A thickset man, at a guess in his late fifties, though he could have been anything from fifty to eighty. Faded blue shirt without a collar. Square, weather-beaten face. One eye-socket blank flesh; out of the other a single small blue eye, flat and without depth, stared at me as if speculating which side I'd have been on at Culloden.

'Like a demon, love possessed me, you obsessed me constantly. What an evil star is mine, that my fate's design should be Je . . . ze . . . be . . . el!'

'Isn't that a hellish noise?' I said.

He considered, head to one side as if listening, then said, 'It's cheery when you're working. And the wife likes it.'

He nodded over his shoulder and I saw on the crown of the hill a low stone building not unlike the one I'd come from.

'She's all for the gramophone,' he said. 'In the navy I liked the wireless. *Workers' Playtime* with Vic Oliver, yon was a great programme.'

'He's married to Churchill's daughter.'

'Do you tell me that?' The single eye regarded me sceptically. 'I thought he was a Jewboy.'

'No idea. I read somewhere he's married to the daughter.'

'That's remarkable. Good for her.' He tucked his chin into his shoulder and sawed at an imaginary fiddle. 'He used to say, "Do you know why I shut my eyes when I'm playing? It's because I don't like to watch folk suffering." ' After a pause, he lowered his hands. 'That always made me laugh.'

It was too late even to smile. Another test failed.

After I left him, the road swung left by a field with half a dozen cows, shaggy brown beasts with long horns which went back in a curving lilt. Past them, it inclined so steeply that I began to pant for every breath of warm air. To my surprise, at the top the narrow road disappeared into the yard of the house I'd seen from below. In the conviction that the farmer should have warned me about a dead end, a kind of indignation carried me forward. As I came to the other end of the farmyard, I looked down a grassy slope to where a rowing boat lay pulled up on the bank of an open stretch of water. It was so quiet that I could hear a lorry, maybe a mile distant, trundling along what had to be a road on the other side of the loch.

I became conscious of a low, steady hissing, which I eventually recognised as the steady turning of a needle at the end of a gramophone record. It came from one of the open windows, and I realised that it was from here the American music had thundered across the countryside. No sign, though, of the farmer's wife. Perhaps that music-lover was making beds; or in hiding under one of them from the intrusion of a stranger. At that last thought, I beat a retreat.

On my way back, I saw the farmer making his way up the field towards the house, followed by an idle string of cows. At sight of me, he swerved and came across.

'The road stops at your house,' I said.

'Nowhere else for it to go.'

'I found that out.'

'So where's your car?' The question seemed irrelevant. As I hesitated, he said. 'You're just taking a walk?'

'That's right.'

'We don't get many folk walking here.'

'I'm staying with your neighbour.'

'Neighbour?'

'Down the road.'

'What brought you there? You know MacLean?'

I shook my head. 'We stopped, looking for something to eat. My mother began to feel unwell, and they put us up.' Then the name MacLean registered. 'I'm talking about the first house down on the right-hand side.'

'So am I.'

'MacLean?'

'Aye, Angus MacLean and his sister. What man would want that, eh? A man needs a bit of a cuddle now and again. You'll not get that from a sister.' He made a face, and went on before I could react. 'The man's in hiding down there. He'd to leave his own island because he was ashamed. He was one of they conchies

– he wouldn't fight for his King – and on that island a lot of the boys didn't come home. Just a worthless kind of a man. He worked in the forestry in Argyll with the other conchies for a while. After the war, he went back to being a schoolmaster again, and then one day the two of them were gone. I was surprised when they turned up here. He must have thought he'd left his past behind him. But it's a small world for a creature like that. I smile to think he has no idea that I know about him. They say the real reason he wouldn't fight was that he favoured yon Hitler man.'

At the beginning, I almost broke in to say, 'It's a mistake – he's South African.' By the end, what stopped me was that I could believe in August as a supporter of the Nazis. But that husband and wife might be brother and sister made no sense to me.

'Are you sure?' I asked. 'If he doesn't know you, how do you know him?'

'I don't,' the man said. He jerked a thumb at the house on the hill above us. 'But *she* does. Oh, she knows him. Any time our paths cross in the town, she dodges away so he'll not see her.'

'Your wife?'

'Island girls make the best wives.' He pulled a wry face. 'Got a temper, though – goes with the red hair. If she heard me, she'd go her duster, call me a damned old gossip, but that's just because he frightens her.'

I offered, 'He's a big man,' not able to keep the question out of my voice, still willing to settle for there being a mistake.

'By Christ, he doesn't frighten *me*.' He poked with his stick at one of the cows that were gathering in a circle round us. 'Anyway, you'd never be such a fool as to say anything to him, eh?'

'I won't say anything.'

'That's all right, then. But why give your money to somebody like that? Now you know the score, you should get out of there.'

'Today if I can.'

On the off chance he might help, I was ready to tell him about the starting motor, but he struck out again at the cow.

'That's the bitch that did it.' He rubbed a finger in his empty eye-socket. 'Hooked me in the face when I was on the milking stool. I cry her Jezebel.'

'But she still has her horns.' Even a town boy knew you could cut off their horns.

'Aye,' he said on a slow outgoing breath, 'but I keep an eye on her now.'

His laugh followed me back down the road.

CHAPTER TWENTY-NINE

Now I had two secrets from Eileen, but could find no chance to share either of them. The first thing I saw when I went in through the gate was August getting out of his car. It was a little battered Austin A30 and he unfolded from it like a man struggling out of a tight jacket.

'It can't be repaired,' he said.

'The starting motor?' I asked stupidly.

He frowned at me. 'It's a good garage. If they say it can't be, it can't be.'

'Did you get a new one?'

No sooner were the words out of my mouth than it occurred to me that he'd been told we'd no money to pay for a repair, never mind a replacement. There might be a fortune in the case in the boot of Eileen's car, but what use was that if I didn't dare let on that it was there?

'No. It's only a small place,' he said.

Panic wiped thoughts of money out of my head. 'But what's going to happen? We can't stay here.'

'They phoned for one while I was there.' He looked at me for a long moment; I couldn't tell what he was thinking. At last, he said, 'What more could they do?'

I couldn't find an answer. It came over me how much I distrusted him. It was too much of a coincidence that the car should have broken down just when we wanted to leave. For all I knew, he'd disabled it and there was nothing wrong with the starting motor. If so, he wouldn't have been near a garage. I couldn't help glancing at the boot of his car. I'd seen him put the starting motor in it that morning. Was it still there?

'Did they say how long it would take?'

'Tell you what, next time I'm in I'll ask them.'

'Could I come with you?'

He rubbed one hand down the length of his chin, studying me, then nodded as if making up his mind to something. 'I don't see why not.'

I went to get into the car.

'What are you doing?' he asked.

'You said I could come.'

'Not now. I'm not going back now.' He made it sound ridiculous.

'What about tomorrow?'

Waiting for him to answer, I understood it was a question to which there were a dozen ways of saying no.

'Tomorrow it is.'

'It's not too soon? Do they get it from Inverness, or does it have to be Glasgow? It doesn't have to be from the factory, does it?' Somewhere in England, I meant.

'It might even have come by tomorrow.' When he bared his teeth in a smile, it was unexpected. 'No harm in hoping.'

He went off then to get on with the work of the day. The errand with the starting motor meant his day was starting late. I expected him to ask me to help, but he didn't. I should have been relieved, but it made me more wary. Maybe he felt he didn't need to keep an eye on me any more. After all, he knew I had been out walking, on my own, no one to stop me. He hadn't asked where I'd been. What mattered was that he'd seen me come back: I had nowhere to go.

Frustratingly, when I went into the kitchen Eileen was with Beate, one on either side of the table, talking over a cup of tea. I told them what August had said about the starting motor. When I'd finished, they drifted back to their conversation. I sipped the tea Beate poured for me, too busy with my thoughts to pay much attention. Eileen was doing most of the talking, and once something she said made Beate smile. It was like a glimpse of a younger and happier woman. As that happened, it occurred to me that we might turn to her for help. I was conscious of how much at ease with each other the two women appeared to be. Because of a man, Beate, too, it seemed to me, had been trapped in a poor kind of life. Sharing that experience with Eileen, it was just possible she might agree to help us. I looked at her as she talked, watched her lips moving, not following the words. Our situation was desperate, and we needed an ally. What made me hesitate was the mad idea that she might be August's sister not his wife.

I needed to talk to Eileen.

The day, however, frittered away without an opportunity. All afternoon, August's chores kept him in the yard, and the house was too small for privacy. When finally Eileen agreed to go walking, Beate, without an invitation or it even being clear who had made the suggestion, came as well. We straggled round the perimeter of the field and the women talked. When I looked over my shoulder, August had come to the corner of the byre and was watching us.

Dinner began as a silent meal. I could find nothing to say. The women's talk had dried up. For once, it was August who broke the silence.

'Working around today, my mind kept turning to where you would look for help if you had a problem. Say, for example, you have to do something. You might not want to do it, it might be a hateful thing, but no matter how you try you can only find one answer. There doesn't seem to be another. I've learned more in my life from books than I ever learned at university. Mostly books I came across on my own.'

'I was desperate to go to university,' Eileen said. 'But my father didn't believe in that for girls, so I went to Jordanhill College to train to be a teacher. He wasn't pleased when I gave it up, and went to be a nurse instead. It got me away from home, though.'

All the time Eileen had been speaking, Beate had been looking across the table at August. Now she asked him, 'Do you remember that landlady you had?' It was as if Eileen hadn't spoken, which made me feel as if she had been insulted. 'It was your first term at university. She came up to waken you, and you called from inside that you were just coming. But because you were only half awake, you didn't speak in English. She thought you were swearing at her!'

Her smile faded as he stared at her in silence.

'You spoke in Afrikaans?' Eileen asked.

'Oh . . . yes,' Beate said.

Don't you mean Gaelic? I wanted to ask. It would be reckless to goad him, but I was sick of their talk of South Africa. As if they were mocking us, it seemed a private game to test our gullibility. I asked, 'Your first language wasn't English?'

'One day the whole world will be talking English,' he said. When he turned his head, the lamplight played on one side of his face, leaving the other in a luminous shadow. 'It's the law of the jungle. Survival of the fittest, Darwin called it. And it's the same for languages. Languages are for buying and selling and winning wars. The weak languages go to the wall. The number of languages will narrow down and down. English beat French. Now it's beaten German. Russian's turn comes next. If an African or a Chink asked me, I'd say learn English.' His voice stayed quiet but became heavier and more emphatic. 'Go where the power is, I'd tell them. Bang your head hard enough against a brick wall, you'll crush your skull. In the end, the whole world will have just the one language to think in.'

'What a horrible world,' Eileen said.

'You're going to talk about culture? Forget about culture. You can translate poetry.'

'I don't think you can.' And she said something I couldn't understand but recognised as French.

He repeated her last words, so lingeringly I could pick them out. '*Luxe, calme et volupté.*'

In his caressing of the words, he seemed to have lost the thread of his argument. His lips moved as if he were saying them over to himself.

'A teacher taught me that. I've never forgotten it. The French wouldn't give that up easily,' Eileen said. 'And won't the Chinese feel the same about the things they love? There are an awful lot of Chinese.' Her tone was lighter as if affected by his response to the poetry she had quoted.

'That's their funeral,' Beate said.

'Try not to be stupid,' August told her.

She frowned at him and said, 'When my grandmother died, they couldn't find her rosary beads. Catholics have to be buried with their rosary beads, so my mother gave hers – she didn't use them. They were put in Grandmother's coffin. The funeral was – on an island; you wouldn't have heard of it. I said to my mother, "Could they not make the funeral later in the day?" "The funerals are always at ten o'clock," she said. They didn't have a hearse, you see, so they used the school bus. It had "School" on the side of it. They dug her grave in the sand, and then they came to a rock base, so they had to build a wooden frame for the grave. It was raining so hard my father said to the priest, "Look, the coffin's floating," so they just had to fill it in right away.'

Eileen was listening with a little frown between her brows. 'This was in South Africa?'

Before Beate could respond, August said, 'The liner we came in from Africa was sunk by a torpedo. From the raft, I watched it go down bow first, heaving up its great behind to dry in the sun while a million sparkling drops showered from it into the sea.'

Beate said, 'If you weren't here, he wouldn't be so polite.'

'Polite?' Eileen shook her head. 'I could see it. It's vivid like a poem. I don't know about polite.'

'He'd have called its arse its arse,' Beate said.

'Oh.'

'But with you here and being a lady . . . What does your husband do?'

Eileen stared at her a moment, then said, 'He owns a factory.'

'I knew you were rich,' Beate said with satisfaction.

'No!' I protested.

They all looked at me.

'*He* may be rich. We're not.'

I didn't dare meet Eileen's eyes. What she thought I was doing, God knows.

August, though, nodded as if it made perfect sense to him that I should claim we were penniless.

'The two of you have run off.' He nodded again and threw up his hands palms upwards. 'Of course.'

Not long afterwards, Eileen went to bed and I was left alone

153

with the pair of them. It was hard to stop thinking of them as husband and wife, but it was hard, too, not to see resemblance between them. He was almost ugly and she wasn't pretty, but there it was – in the nose and the shape of the eyes. If I'd just met them and been told they were brother and sister, I would have said, yes, I could see it: the family resemblance.

When I was alone, I lay awake under the blanket on the couch. In my thoughts August went by the name he had given me, but it was as if now another man stood behind him in the shadows; and Angus frightened me more than August ever had, for if he existed he lived a hard life in a remote place to hide a guilty secret. He was an educated man with half a shelf of books. A man full of ideas with no one to discuss them with. The truth is, if Angus existed, he was poor and needed to be rich. How could he know the money was in the case, and not want to have it? But how could he get it, be able to keep it, be sure of going unpunished, if Eileen and I were alive? I could believe the act of murder might be a horror to him. But how could he give up the money? I could see how the days might pass while he tried to make up his mind.

CHAPTER THIRTY

I woke with the thought that Beate wouldn't allow anything to happen to Eileen. Eyes shut, I listened to the sounds of movement. Water ran. There was the rattle of a pot being laid on the iron stove. I made up my mind to speak to her.

But when I sat up on the edge of the bed it was August who was standing by the stove, stirring the pot.

'Beate's gone to take the eggs from under the hen,' he said. 'And there's porridge on the go.'

I'd never seen him lift a hand to help inside the house. I stood and put on a shirt over the vest I'd worn to sleep in; then pulled on my trousers and zipped up. When I turned, he was watching me. 'Beate told me you were a modest boy.'

The half-smile that accompanied the words completed my uneasiness. It took an effort to go over beside him to the cupboard where the bowls were kept.

'Do you want one, too?'

'I'll breakfast with you,' he said.

I put a bowl on either side of the table. He poured porridge into them, almost filling each one. It was far more than I had taken on the other mornings. When I put milk in, my bowl was full to overflowing. He went back to the cupboard and fetched a third bowl, poured milk into it and set it beside his other one. Then he started to eat, spooning up porridge and milk in turns. I scattered salt on mine and began.

'It's a pity the hives aren't ready,' he said. 'Some honey goes well with porridge. Often and often enough, my father told me he despised that, but it didn't stop me – I've always had a sweet tooth. Now that he's dead, I can't help being sorry I defied him. What harm would the salt have done me?'

Porridge and a battle over whether or not it should be

sweetened. That sounded like the childhood of someone called Angus, a countryman of mine. His pause seemed to challenge me to comment as if he read my thoughts. I said nothing.

'What kind of factory is it?' he asked.

The spoon paused halfway to my mouth.

'This factory your father owns? What does it make?'

'I wouldn't call it a factory. More like a workshop than a factory. Small stuff.'

Yes, but what exactly? I waited for him to ask. I'm a poor liar; my mind had gone blank. As he watched me, head to one side, I felt sweat run down my back.

Leaning forward, he asked, 'What made you run off?'

I stammered, 'It – it's not something I want to talk about.'

'Some people would preach about putting up with what a father does, however bad it is. But some things are hard to put up with. A bad father.' His tongue was fat and red as he licked the spoon. 'A bad husband. Better out than in, get it off your chest. I'm a good listener.'

After an endless waiting, he pushed back his chair. I took it as a release and got to my feet.

'Don't let me keep you back,' I said. 'You're late this morning.'

'No, I'm early. I've done what had to be done.' He piled one bowl into the other. 'Soon as we're finished, we can go.'

'Go where?'

He looked at me as if I was stupid, and of course the answer was obvious. Go to town. Where else? He put the bowls in the sink and sat down again. After a moment, I took my place opposite him.

Beate came back with the eggs. It was strange. Everything was so normal. The eggs were boiled and we ate them with butter and salt and drank tea. All the time the two of them talked, just a few words back and forward, with more missed out than said, as people do when they've known each other all their lives. They even smiled at the same moment and once laughed together. I might as well have been invisible. Desperately, I wanted Eileen to be there, but it was just eight in the morning and she had slept heavily since her illness.

There was still no sign of her when we set out.

August was cramped in the car, crouched down turning the wheel with one hand, his shoulder rubbing against mine though I sat over as far as I could. 'I'll take a guess,' he said. 'If *your* father had been South African, he'd have been in the Broederbond. One of the old ones behind the scenes pulling the strings. You get them in every country. Here as well, but there's no name for them here.'

'Masons?'

'Playing at it,' he said scornfully. 'Not the same thing at all.' After that, he never said a word or spared a glance from the tortuous narrow road.

In the early-morning light, the town looked prosperous and smug. All the buildings were of stone, cream stone and two different shades of brown, each sharp-cut rectangle so new and clean it might have been freshly scrubbed. There was a long stripe of grass on either side of the main street with parking spaces facing into the pavement. We stopped in front of a building that looked as if it must once have been a rich man's house; it had steps up to its front door and a Bank of Scotland sign. To the side there was a shop with an enormous glass window with a display of long tartan skirts.

'I won't be long,' August said.

I watched until he went round the corner. He walked very upright and swung his arms as if keeping step to a marching song. It was so quiet I heard a little broken sighing sound. It was my own breath, coming hard as if I had been running. A man went by with his jacket over his arm. As he passed, he broke step and stared in at me. I wondered if he had expected to see August, and somehow the idea of anyone knowing August surprised me. Anyway, after the briefest hesitation he walked on. Maybe it was just that he had thought the cars were empty, then sensed he was being observed from one of them. I thought about getting out. I listened to my breath slowing. After a time, a stout man in a blue suit went up the steps of the bank, unlocked the front door and went inside. Shortly afterwards, two younger men arrived, staff, I supposed; the day's business of the small town beginning.

I got out of the car and walked slowly in the direction August had gone. Before the corner, there were half a dozen shops, a butcher, a window full of balls of wool, a little café with net curtains and a hand-printed card taped to the door. I read slowly down the list of prices: eggs and bacon and ham salad and cakes and tea. Behind the curtain I could make out the shape of a woman with a fistful of cutlery going from table to table as slowly as a diver groping across an ocean floor.

From the corner the side street ran down past a building with posters by the door about the importance of pregnant mothers collecting their ration of cod liver oil and orange juice, a row of bungalows with cropped lawns and rose bushes, a square stone house with its name worked into the iron gate: Tigh-na-mara. At the bottom, there was a path by a river with a little island in the middle and trees hanging their branches down towards the water. I stood there for a bit, watching two swans sail along on top of their reflections, then retraced my steps.

As I came back on to the main street, I saw August approaching the car from the other direction. He was carrying a large metal can, which he put into the boot.

Slamming the lid, he said, 'Two birds with one stone. We were needing oil for the lamps.'

'I'm sorry I left the car.'

'What's to be sorry about?'

'Unlocked, I mean.'

'It makes no difference. You could leave it for a week here and no one would touch it. Tell you what.' He pulled a key ring from his pocket and gave it a long, considering look, and then turned one of the keys in the lock of the boot. 'That should keep my oil safe.' He was laughing at me.

'Can we go to the garage now?' I asked.

When he started across the road, I thought that was where we were going; but when I caught up with him, he said, 'Since we're here anyway, we could buy beans. I forgot beans yesterday.'

I followed him into the grocer's and stood by as he bought beans and a packet of custard creams and a box of chocolate biscuits, a pot of jam and one of thick-slice orange marmalade, and half a dozen bars of fudge.

Outside, he handed me the bags of groceries and the key ring and said, 'Put these in the boot.'

As he turned away, I said, 'Are you going to the garage?'

I was determined to go with him.

'Give it till Monday, they said.'

'What?'

I caught him by the upper arm, the muscle hard as stone. He frowned down at my hand and I took it away.

'I asked about your starting motor when I was getting oil for the lamps. Now I feel the sweet tooth needs feeding. Yesterday I resisted temptation. Today I don't. So you could say it's your fault.'

I followed him along the pavement. He stopped at a window set with pastries on trays and mounds of soft rolls in one corner.

'When you don't have much money, treats are few and far between,' he said, not removing his gaze from the window. 'But Beate will understand this one. I'll say to her, "The time's come for treating ourselves. Get used to it."' He smiled as if he had made a joke and I thought the smile, like everything about him, was false. Only the greed with which he stared into the window seemed genuine. 'Meringues. Eclairs. Even the words make your mouth water. Go over and wait for me. I'll not be a minute.' As I turned away, he murmured, 'I like to take my time choosing.'

Clutching the two bags in the curve of one arm, I opened the boot. When I was in the car, I sat looking at the ring in my hand. It had two keys. One had opened the boot.

After a moment, I lifted myself across into the driver's seat, put the other key in the ignition and started the engine.

As I drove away, August ran from the baker's shop.

I didn't look back.

BOOK FOUR

The Deep Pool

CHAPTER THIRTY-ONE

August had told me money was scarce. Maybe that was why he hadn't filled the petrol tank. I was fifty miles down the road before it occurred to me I should check. When I did, it seemed that officially the tank was empty. The car kept moving, the engine made the same noise as before, but now I knew every second was the one before it stopped.

Before it did, a petrol pump appeared. Just the one, alone outside a shop in the village I was running through.

A man came out of the shop and unscrewed the cap. 'How much?'

For a moment, I thought he was asking how much money I had. Answer: almost none; certainly not enough to pay for the petrol I was going to need to get me where, without having thought about it or decided anything, I knew I should go.

'Fill her up. Please.'

The pump wheezed like an asthmatic and I imagined the hiss of petrol falling into the tank.

'Is there a Gents?' I asked.

'Sorry.' He stood with one shoulder lower than the other, staring down at the nozzle in his hand.

'Bloody hell,' I said mournfully.

He gave me a considering look as if assessing my need.

'There's one in the shop. Not for the public. Tell the girl I said it was all right.'

It was a narrow cubicle beside the storeroom. It smelled of cigarettes and disinfectant. I unzipped and stood over the bowl. Unlike the pump nozzle nothing flowed. I put my cock away again and went out into the shop.

The man was back serving behind the counter. As he reached up to get a packet of cereal from the shelf, I walked out of the shop. The girl who had told me where the lavatory was smiled and nodded as I went past. Presumably, it didn't occur to her that I hadn't paid.

The car was sitting at the pump. I got in and drove away.

It had been kind of the man to let me use the shop toilet.

As I'd overheard August say to Beate that morning, Good deeds can have bad consequences.

CHAPTER THIRTY-TWO

The smell wasn't pleasant. Close up, it made its individual contribution to the general background of smells that had filled my nose the moment I went through the entrance. It came from a man with two dead flies caught in his hair, who was mopping the entrance hall. He must have seen the direction of my glance for he swiped a hand through his hair dislodging one fly and missing the other. He pointed above his left shoulder and I saw a thickly encrusted flypaper. 'You've to be careful,' he said. 'They hang them all over the place.'

It was hard to tell his age; somewhere between fifty and a hundred; a wizened man who had seen too much. It was disconcerting to have him look at me with contempt.

'Tommy? You're Tommy Glass's son?' He wiped a hand down his mouth in the rubbing gesture of an alcoholic. 'You ever hear of Hart Danks? Naw? Well, *I*'ve heard of him. He wrote "Silver Threads among the Gold" – about his mother. A great fucking wee song. And he died in a rooming hoose in New York. You know what the note he left said?'

I shook my head.

' "It's hard to die alone." Right? And your father's not here, by the way.'

'I was told he was.'

'Oh, he was. I said he's not now. He's in the hospital.'

'Which one?'

'Nae idea. But I asked after him. He's in a hell of a bad way.'

He took me by the arm and drew me after him down the corridor into a room not much larger than a cubicle, which I tried hard not to see properly.

'I wisnae there when he keeled over. Went out for a pie and he was away in the ambulance by the time I got back. Soon as I heard, I got this before some bastard nicked it.' He pulled a cardboard shoebox from under the bed. 'If you're his son, you should have it. If you want it, that is?'

Maybe he suspected I'd refuse and confirm his poor opinion of me. Instead, I tucked it under my arm.

'He didn't have much to say for himself, but he talked to me. He was in the army, you ken?'

I nodded.

'He was in a reserved occupation, tae.'

'Working a forklift on the docks.' I remembered.

'Like I said, he didnae have to go. His missus stayed out half the night with some bloke so the bloody fool packed it in and got called up. Finished up in the Sappers. He got tae France on D-Day plus three, he said. But no for long. He stood on a shrapnel mine in a back alley in Cannes and they shipped him back home. Finished up at a convalescent camp in Stoke-on-Trent.'

'I didn't know any of that.'

'Like I say, he talked to me. We used to have some great arguments.'

He trailed after me through the hall.

Outside I clutched the box under my arm and hovered, wanting to escape.

'Maybe you should know Tommy's all for being cremated. I'll tell you something he said to me one time. He said, "If there is a God, his heid'll fall off wi shaking it at human stupidity."' He gave me a final glance of dislike and went back inside.

The young doctor at the hospital didn't think much of me, either. It was, apparently, six weeks since my father's stroke.

'Although,' the doctor said, 'the likely thing is that he'd had a series of pinprick strokes before that.'

When they brought him in, things had been complicated by the fact he was suffering from malnutrition and tuberculosis.

I stood at the end of the bed, trying to match this stranger against a memory. He was a skeletal man, who had been a lean man. A still man, who had never been still except with a book in his hand.

Because I was hungry, I went to the canteen. I bought a bacon roll and a cup of tea from the volunteer woman, and then found I had no appetite. After one bite, I pushed the roll aside, sat the shoebox on the table and took off the lid. There was nothing in it, just rubbish. Not a diary or a letter or a last will and testament, not even a postcard. He'd used it for storing newspaper clippings. At a cursory glance, there was no rhyme or reason to the collection. When I had time, I would go through it and try to understand why he might have chosen these things. I unfolded the birthday card my mother had given me, on which my father had written his address, and laid it on top of the cuttings and put the lid back on the box. It was possible he had sent the card as a cry for help. If so, no one had come to his rescue, no knight in shining armour. I sipped the tea and listened to the clatter of cups and voices, music from a wireless, the clatter of a dropped plate.

When I went back he was dead. 'Without recovering consciousness', as they say. No one had thought to come and look for me.

CHAPTER THIRTY-THREE

The secretary's eyes rested on me a moment and then widened. In the instant before she recognised me, she had the same air of indifference and self-possession that had irritated and impressed me on my first day at the factory. In those widened eyes, I saw alarm and excitement.

'My name's Harry Glass.'

'I know who you are.'

I tried, but couldn't remember her name.

'Did he get you?' she asked. 'The . . . the man who phoned here after you left asking for your address?'

Remembering the little wrestler threatening me in my mother's house, I nodded. 'Not right away, but he found me,' I said.

'He's dead,' she said. 'Is that why you've come back?'

'Mr Bernard's dead?' I stared at her in shock.

'Of course not.' That came out with the old arrogance, and I remembered that her name was Theresa. 'Mr Shea. He was a business acquaintance of Mr Bernard's.'

'The man who wanted my address?'

She nodded.

The little Glasgow gangster.

'He's dead?'

'It was in the papers.' She studied me and I could see her thinking. 'You didn't see it? I thought that's why you'd come back.'

I wondered how much she knew or guessed of Morton's business.

'I want to speak to Mr Bernard,' I said.

She licked her lips. 'Is *she* with you?'

She meant Eileen. Something in her tone brought a vivid

image of that tight behind waggling for Bernard Morton. As surely as if I'd seen them, I knew she'd been bedded by Morton. Perhaps his wife's disappearance had given her hope of becoming wife number two. It took me by surprise how much I was offended by her calling Eileen '*she*'.

Heading for the stairs, I said over my shoulder, 'Mrs Morton isn't with me.'

She came after me in a clacking of heels, brushed past and led the way. As we passed the first door on the landing, I glanced inside, half expecting to see the fat older brother on his haunches in front of the filing cabinet. The room was empty.

She knocked and in the same movement opened the door.

In a voice husky with excitement, she said, 'Someone to see you.'

Morton was behind his desk with a pile of papers in front of him. He glanced at me and then said to her, 'Get out!'

She made an odd clicking in her throat and hung in place as if suspended on a hook for a long helpless moment.

As the door closed behind her, he capped the pen he'd been using. From the moment I appeared he hadn't taken his eyes from me.

'Have you been doing the hokey-cokey with my wife?' he asked, his voice quiet and reasonable.

'*What?*'

'You know. You put your middle leg in, You take your middle leg out, You put your middle leg in, And you shake it all about.'

What answer was there to that? I could only think of one.

'I found the money,' I said.

'Where is she?' He looked at the door as if expecting her to appear.

'Where the money is.'

'In that case,' he said, 'we should go and see Norman.'

He put his closed fists on the desk and levered himself up, never taking his eyes from my face. It came over me with a chill how little the money concerned him.

CHAPTER THIRTY-FOUR

Bernard's home in Giffnock, an old solid house of stone, had been his father's and maybe his grandfather's. I don't know why it had gone to him, the younger son. Maybe because he was married, and it had appeared as if Norman would never marry. That could have been their father's way of marking his disappointment.

Anyway, when we left the factory it was for the other side of the city from Giffnock. I tried to talk to Morton in the car, but he shut me up. After that, I sat and watched the trees and terraces of Great Western Road flicker past. Off the main road, we went by an allotment with sheds and a glimpse of turned earth and overgrown rhubarb. It looked neglected, as if there was no need any more to dig for victory. Just beyond it, Morton pulled into the visitors' parking area in front of a block of flats. There was grass in front, so new you could still see the lines where the turf had been laid, and low bushes and a few straggling lanky trees.

The hall was carpeted just as if it was the entry to a private house, and there were plants in big pots by the lift that took us in a silent rush up to the sixth floor. When its door slid back, I saw fat Norman the bookkeeper waiting for us. Since his was the only entrance, I understood his flat must take up the whole floor.

'I didn't believe it,' he said, patting his lips as he looked at me.

Bernard grunted and, putting his hand in the small of my back, urged me out of the lift. The mild, insistent pressure disconcerted me like sudden heat from the folding back of a furnace door.

One brother in front, the other almost tramping on my heels, I went into a room that stretched to French windows at the far end. Without a word to me, the two brothers went outside. Apart from films, I'd hardly ever seen the inside of a room with a balcony.

Because the glass doors had been slid shut, I couldn't hear a word, but they were leaning close, faces inches apart; it looked like an argument. To my surprise, Norman was doing most of the talking. When he turned his head to stare at me, I beat a retreat back into the middle of the room. The long walls on either side were lined with paintings, big and small, twenty or more of them. For an unreal moment I felt like a schoolboy again and saw Miss McAlester, not much more than a girl herself, throat flushing as she herded us through the art gallery at Kelvingrove. It only lasted for a moment, but it was very vivid, a kind of displacement, I suppose, for the fear I was in.

Next moment, the glass door was pushed open.

Norman came in ahead of his brother. He held himself differently from the man I'd met before. Even his voice was different. His asthmatic wheezing now sounded in my ears like the panting of an animal. Whatever had happened, he wasn't apologising any more for his existence.

'Don't stand there,' he said.

My heart juddered.

He took a moment as if savouring my bewilderment.

'It took me a long time to get that clean,' he said.

I was standing almost in the middle of a roughly shaped circle. It made a patch of lightness on the dark blue of the carpet as if it had been soaked and bleached and scrubbed.

'For God's sake, Norman,' his brother said.

'I'm just asking him to move.'

Not knowing why, I stepped to the side. Getting off the circle put me hard against the couch.

'Don't sit down there,' Norman said. 'I had to clean that as well.'

On the blue leather, I saw similar faded patches. For some reason, as I raised my eyes they settled on the painting hung above the couch. It showed an old man cradling a dog, but the dog had the face of a man and the man the grey muzzle of a dog.

Norman came to my side. For a big man, he moved quickly.

'Oh, dear,' he said. 'How did I miss those?'

The glass of the painting was covered with dark brown flecks.

Instead of complaining again Bernard crossed to stand on the other side of me.

'Fuck!' His voice was just above a whisper, and I was alarmed to see that his face had gone grey.

'That would be the *mot juste*,' Norman said cheerfully.

Bernard turned away and sat down. He sank forward, head in his hands. 'I shouldn't have brought him here,' he said.

Norman had one knee on the couch and was leaning forward to pick delicately with his thumbnail at one of the flecks on the glass. 'I wouldn't have believed it. I love Colquhoun. And over there's a MacBryde. Such dear friends, I thought it would be nice to let them face one another. And I simply didn't see these.' Scratching at the last trace of the fleck. 'It shows that you should move paintings around or you stop seeing them, even the ones you love.'

With a sigh, he wriggled his bulk round and settled on the couch. I was left standing between the two brothers.

'You've caused more trouble than you could imagine,' Norman said.

'None of it was—'

'Eileen's fault? So why isn't she here with you?'

That took a long time to explain. I told them everything I could think of, except what the old crofter had told me about August's real name and his relationship to Beate. When I was confused, Norman would ask one question and then another until things were clear to him. Bernard's head came up but he didn't say anything. Only, as I went on, the grey in his cheeks was replaced by a flush of blood.

'So you left the poor man,' Norman said at last, 'with nothing to show for his morning but a bag of pastries. Unless, of course, he ate them as he walked home.' He shook his head at me. 'You have a weakness for stealing cars.'

Incongruously, I thought of August's car left behind in the yard at the factory; biscuits, jam, marmalade and half a dozen bars of fudge in the boot. And something else, besides: the box of newspaper clippings. If they held a clue as to who my father had

been and what he had made of the world, they were gone. I
didn't suppose I would ever see them again.

'You dirty little bastard,' Bernard said. They were his first
words in half an hour. 'You ran away and left her.'

CHAPTER THIRTY-FIVE

Before Norman insisted that we stop for something to eat, I sat in the back of the car on my own. That first part of the journey passed mostly in silence. It was as if the brothers, having decided to ignore me, had nothing to say to each other. As for me, I had done all I could and everything was out of my hands. My eyelids kept closing and I had difficulty staying awake. In a strange way, I was at peace with myself. It wasn't true that I had run away, for I was going back. I hadn't deserted Eileen. I'd done the only thing I could think of to bring her help. I'd told Bernard that Beate wouldn't let August hurt her, and I believed that. Whatever happened to her now, and to me, would be decided by others.

Tired of Norman's complaining of hunger, Bernard stopped abruptly as we ran through a small town.

'Where's this?' I asked in the car park of the hotel, and Norman grunted, 'Pitlochry.'

He had mutton broth, then a steak pie, pushing aside the vegetables and asking for more potatoes to add to the half-dozen already on the plate; afterwards he crammed in a pudding. Watching him sweat, chins quivering as he shovelled it in, made me feel sick, but didn't stop me finishing a plate of haddock and chips. As for Bernard, he emptied a pot of coffee while he waited for us, and had a brandy with each of his last two cups.

In the middle of his meal, spraying flecks of pastry as he spoke, Norman assured me suddenly, 'You did the right thing.'

What could I say in reply that wouldn't be ridiculous? I hope so?

'You got in over your head, and now you want to make everything all right again. I understand that.'

Gloomy Bernard pushed away his plate of uneaten food.

'And that's how it's going to be,' Norman said. 'Eileen's had her fling and we'll take her home. It'll be as if it never happened. She's been strange for a long time.'

Staring at the table, Bernard said, 'She lost a child.'

'Alice,' I said.

When he glanced up, I saw that he hated me, but his head went down again so quickly it wasn't hard to think I might be mistaken. 'After the child died, she blamed herself and wanted to be punished. If I punished her, it was what she wanted.'

'She didn't need that,' I blurted. I alarmed myself, but as much out of shame as courage went on, 'Whatever she needed, she didn't need that.'

'A boy . . . How would you understand?'

'It's not difficult. All it would take is to be a decent human being.'

'She tried to commit suicide. More than once. I kept her where I could keep an eye on her.'

'Everything just as it was before,' Norman said. I saw the dark wad of food churning in his open mouth as he chewed. 'Except that I don't think we could see our way to giving you your old job back.' He giggled. 'Sorry.'

I hadn't thought any of it through properly. I'd wanted to make Eileen safe, and I couldn't do that by myself. But if I'd gone to the police, what could I have told them? That we'd stolen money and a man who had given us shelter might or might not have seen it? But if I arrived with the Morton brothers, August couldn't do anything against three of us. That was the way my mind had worked. Now, as the muddle cleared, I asked myself the obvious question.

If they drove away with Eileen, what would happen to me?

CHAPTER THIRTY-SIX

When we left the hotel, Norman came into the back seat beside me. God knows why. Because Bernard was so silent? Because he wanted to taunt his brother? Because he sensed how unpleasant it was for me to be close to him? He came in beside me for one of those reasons, or for some other I didn't even want to think about. From time to time, his leg brushed against mine, and there was no escape from the greasy warmth of his breath. There was a darkness in him. I had discovered that; too late, perhaps.

When I couldn't stand the silence any longer, I said, 'August is a dangerous man. I don't know if I made that clear.'

What was I doing? Asking that they wouldn't go off and leave me with him? Was I pleading? I gathered the scraps of my pride around me and closed my mouth tight.

'It had better still be there,' Norman said.

It took me a moment to realise he was talking about the money.

'Where did it come from?' If I was going to get hurt because of it, why shouldn't I know?

At first I thought he wasn't going to answer, but then he said, 'It was Mr Shea's money.'

'How could it be?' I had thought of him as a little street thug, someone you hired.

'Who says crime doesn't pay?'

Cutting across Norman's high-pitched giggle, Bernard snarled over his shoulder, 'Leave it!'

Norman, however, was in no mood for taking orders.

'Certainly I wouldn't know where that money of his came from – best not to know.' He paused an instant as if inviting a protest, but Bernard had sunk back into silence. 'Bernard met him first through a mutual acquaintance. He was interested in politics, would you believe? And even more against trade unions and all that sort of thing than my brother is. The two of them did some things together, and I was informed but not entirely *involved*.' The same giggle burst from him, an overspilling of some mysterious source of high spirits.

'Anyway, when the big thing came along, we were, you could say, overstretched. Out of our depth, more or less. Put it this way, we didn't have what was needed to pull the last lever we needed to pull. And there he was, ready to help, for a not entirely fair share of the rewards. Mr Shea and his case of money. It had to be ready cash, the gentleman we were dealing with insisted on that. He'd been out in Kenya governing the niggers for so long he'd got into their way of doing business. But when he saw the money, he refused to take the case! It seems Mr Shea kept his money in the Clydesdale Bank.' He tapped me on the arm, 'You understand? Clydesdale Bank notes offered to an English gentleman. He thought Shea had printed them himself. To be fair – it's important to be fair, isn't it? – Bernard was magnificent at calming things down. He promised the notes would be exchanged for Bank of England notes. The gentleman was placated – not difficult since he didn't want to lose his bribe. The only thing he insisted on was that Bernard make the exchange. And Shea let my brother have the case to complete the transaction. It shows how an English gentleman taking a high line can upset the Sheas of this world. That seemed to be that. Everything back on track. And then you came along.' He sighed and said sorrowfully, 'What on earth were you thinking of?'

Driving the car away with Eileen beside me was an event in the distant past. An archaeologist digging into prehistory might be able to tell something had been built on a particular spot, but not why. After a time, there was nothing but guesses.

I shook my head.

'Anyway, Mr Shea wasn't in the best of tempers when he came back empty-handed from chasing you. Unfortunately, his solution was that we should pay him what he'd lost. He couldn't see it was a problem we all shared.'

'Shea's dead,' I said. 'The receptionist, Theresa, told me.'

'Didn't you see it in the papers?'

'I haven't seen a paper in a while.'

'They made quite a splash of it. It was on the wireless, too – not just the Scottish news, the one from London as well.' As the car took a corner at speed, the fat leg nudged mine. 'He was found at three in the morning lying in the middle of the road outside the Stevenson Memorial Church in Belmont Street. It took some time to identify him, for there wasn't much of his face left. Although his head had been beaten to a pulp, there was no blood, which meant he'd been brought there after he was killed. The police decided he'd probably been dumped from a car. They wanted to know if anyone had seen a car stopping at the church after midnight. If he was killed indoors, they said, the room must have been covered in blood. Halfway up the walls, they said. We'd to keep our eyes open. Lots of appeals like that. But he was such a bad man, I doubt if they're looking too hard. The Deputy Chief Constable himself told me – this was after his third malt – Shea was responsible for four killings they couldn't prove. People were too afraid of him to testify, he explained. Do you know what he told me then?'

He waited until I admitted I didn't know.

'Whoever killed that bastard should be given the freedom of the city.' He could hardly get the words out for giggling.

CHAPTER THIRTY-SEVEN

For almost two hours I'd been in the front seat beside Bernard with my nose pressed against the window. I couldn't read a map but, starting from Inverness, it turned out that I had a good memory for the sequence of roads Eileen and I had taken and, at certain moments of doubt, an excellent one for images of the landscape, which culminated at last in a perspective of mountains ahead, making me ask Bernard to turn into a minor road on the right.

The difficulty came with the network of back roads we then found ourselves in. Over and over again, I was faced with the choice of turning left or right as narrow roads came to junctions or split off, more than once ending in a farm track. Through all this the two brothers were surprisingly quiet, but the temperature climbed until sweat ran down my back. The only thing I could think was that I'd reacted to the first glimpse of the mountains and turned off the main road too soon. It didn't help that as the minutes passed Bernard's speed rose so that whenever he stamped on the brakes to surge round a corner the wood of hedges rattled against the window beside me.

We were past before it registered.

'That's it! The sign I told you about!'

I twisted round to look back and he hit the brake so hard my side was battered against the dashboard. He put down his window and, leaning out, reversed in the dark. We'd passed the post going the wrong way. Now, reversed beyond the opening, the headlamps still shone on the back of the sign; but when, rubbing my bruised kidney, I got out to check I could just make out the crude daub done, August had told me, by his sister: SNACKS. We were there. For better or worse.

There was no attempt to conceal our arrival. As Bernard

swung into the yard, our lights flooded across the front of the house. He pulled in behind Eileen's car, still in the same place outside the shed in which the pig had been killed. Before the engine was switched off, Norman had heaved himself out. As I came beside him, he was fiddling at the boot with the key I'd given him.

'You didn't lock it,' he said and lifted the lid.

I was sure I had, but there was no point in arguing. There wasn't anything to say. The case wasn't there.

Bernard was already walking towards the house. Before he got to the door, it opened and Eileen stood in the entrance. They exchanged words, but though I'd started towards them their voices were too low for me to hear what was said. She turned and he followed her inside.

Coming into the room, over Bernard's shoulder I saw Eileen sitting down again at the table, where a place was set for her. August was already seated opposite her, a plateful of food half eaten in front of him. Beate was leaning back against the sink, as if she'd turned from her work at the interruption. For an instant, it held composed and still as a painting and then Norman burst in behind me.

'I'll put the police on you. Where's the phone?' he cried.

'We don't have one,' August said. His voice was that of a man from the islands, lilting and apologetic. Sitting at the table, shoulders bowed, slumped over his food, he seemed much smaller than before.

'Has there been an accident?' Beate asked.

Ignoring them, Norman pushed past us to the table.

'The case isn't in the car,' he wheezed down at Eileen.

'What case?' she said. Without giving him time to answer, she asked Bernard, 'A case?' She made it sound like a bag of dogshit. 'Is that why you're here?'

The two brothers spoke at the same time. Bernard's mono-syllable was lost in Norman's outburst of anger. 'Are you telling me you don't know where it is?'

'Who *are* these people?' Beate asked.

Oddly enough, her question was directed at August. Perhaps

she was in the habit of expecting him to know everything. He shrugged and stared down at the table, seeming to try to distance himself from all of us.

'I'm the husband,' Bernard said. 'I've come to take my wife home.'

Then an extraordinary thing happened. Eileen looked at me and then at him, and she shook her head. I couldn't know that the moment had changed my life, but something beyond the mind understood for my heart moved in me.

She had made a choice between us. He, too, saw that and understood what it meant. For that moment, it was as if the three of us were alone.

'Mr Gas?' he wondered. The words were dry with contempt, like a stick that was ready to break, but there was no disbelief in them. 'A boy who ran away because he was frightened.'

'But he came back.' She spoke quietly, but with an extra-ordinary soft vehemence.

Was that enough to make her love me? It was a choice I had hardly considered, and now it had been made for me.

Norman, however, was not to be turned from his own concern. 'Where's it gone?'

'She doesn't know,' I said.

He overshadowed her with his bulk. 'Either you know or he does. Which is it? Is it the boy? Is he the liar?' He turned on me. 'Are you the liar?'

'And if he is,' Beate cried, 'hasn't a son the right to protect his mother?'

At that, I heard a peculiar click in Bernard's throat as if the dry stick were being snapped in two.

'A son.' He hitched himself with one haunch on the table, looking down on Eileen. 'Well, we always wanted one of those.'

He looked from her to me, and the heaves of his laughter broke like a tidal wave. It promised us a lifetime of scorn, of hurtful misunderstandings, side-glances, sneers, jokes and asides, all the pain of the mismatched, unmatchable years. We stood under it and weren't parted. And when it ended, we had survived it and he saw that we had survived it.

The room put together the broken pieces of its silence. I became conscious of Beate frowning and smiling strangely in her confusion; and that August, even if he didn't understand everything, had caught the central fact of the relation between Eileen and me.

Only Norman was unaffected. He had waited the laughter out, let it flow round him, and now went straight on.

'That case belongs to me – to us, my brother and me. We want it back.'

'I don't know where it is,' I said.

As I spoke, my eyes turned to August. As soon as I'd done it, I knew that it must seem like an accusation. Certainly, I didn't do it deliberately. If there had been a moment of thought, I wouldn't have risked it. In anticipation perhaps, he had raised his head and met my look blankly, almost vacantly.

'If you think I'll leave without that case, you'll make me do damage,' Norman said. 'I'll not be cheated.'

August sighed. It was a quiet sound after so much noise, but it made its mark.

'I meant no harm,' he said. 'I couldn't understand why it was left locked up out there. Why wasn't it brought into the house? So I took it out and found a hiding place for it. I've never done anything like that in my life before. But that's all I did. I didn't even look inside it.' His voice was dull, like that of a man full of guilt and self-blame. When he went on, it was almost in a whine. 'There's no living to be made in a place like this.' He put his head in his hands and began to weep.

I looked at him with something like horror.

'Let's go get it,' Norman said. To Bernard, he said, 'You stay here and sort out this pair.'

'Not on your own,' Bernard said. 'The two of us'll go.'

'You not trust me?'

'What are you talking about?' Bernard sounded bewildered.

Norman stared at him, eyes blinking constantly. He must have understood that the idea of being deserted for the money had never entered his brother's head.

'All I meant was I can do it myself. You know I can. See what I brought?' With a struggle – maybe it was held by the fat of his belly – he pulled a gun from under his jacket. Waving it at us, he said, 'Don't worry about it working. I got it from a friend of ours.' He giggled. 'He doesn't need it any more.'

At sight of the gun, August put his forehead down on the table and covered his head with his arms. It was ignominious.

Norman waddled behind him and poked him in the neck with the gun.

'Monkeys do that,' he said, grinning at his brother over the crouching man. 'It means: my arse is yours.' He poked again, the gun gouging into flesh. 'Stand up!'

August lurched to his feet, but bowed forward, leaning on the table as if his legs could hardly support him.

'Where is it?' the fat man shouted, his voice breaking with excitement. His eyes went round the room. 'Where have you hidden it?'

'Outside,' August mumbled.

'What? What?'

'I dug a hole under a rock.'

'Show me, you bastard!'

August began to move towards the door. Panting for breath, Norman crowded after him. The gun jabbed and jabbed. August showed no sign of feeling it.

'Don't think I wouldn't kill you,' Norman said. There was a euphoria about him that reminded me of my friend Tony the morning after he claimed to have lost his virginity.

Bernard said suddenly, 'Something's wrong.'

He moved in front of them, blocking August. Till that moment his features had been blurred, now they were sharp, wary and suspicious. It was as if he had come awake.

Catching August by the chin, forcing his head up, he asked, 'Why hide it outside?'

But it was Norman who answered. Voice shrill and breaking, he cried, 'Because he was frightened.'

'Tell us again,' Bernard insisted. 'Where's the money?'

'Under a rock by a pool,' August said.

Bernard slapped him in the face. The act was horrifying but the reaction was worse, for August whimpered.

'Tell us where! We'll find it ourselves.'

'And leave him here?' Norman sneered. 'Where's the sense in that?' It seemed his brother becoming active was an unwelcome development.

Bernard ignored him. 'We could shoot you in the legs,' he told August. 'That would keep you here till we came back.'

'Please,' August begged. 'You wouldn't find it in the dark.'

'We've got all night.'

Norman lost patience at this. He shoved August so that he staggered forward, causing Bernard instinctively to step aside. As he did, August moved out into the hall and opened the outside door. Next moment, as if he had tugged the brothers in his wake, all three were gone.

CHAPTER THIRTY-EIGHT

I didn't so much sit down as collapse into a chair opposite Eileen, my legs giving way under me. Next moment, I was lifted to my feet by the sound of a car coughing into life. When I went outside, there were no clouds and the sky was full of stars.

A figure coming to my side startled me. The height, almost the same as mine, told me it was Beate.

'They've taken their car,' I said. The low note of the engine grumbled along, not fading at all. 'Why would they take a car?'

'The fat one was in a hurry. He had no time to waste.'

Though she stood close enough to make me uncomfortable, she kept her face turned from me as she spoke.

'August said he'd hidden the case under a rock near a pool.' She didn't answer. 'There's just the one pool near here, isn't there?'

I could hear the sigh of her breath, feel its warmth on my cheek. She was so close I caught her smell, not very clean, but mixed with a salty, heavy warmth.

'Why didn't August take them by the path?' I persisted.

'Maybe he tried,' she said softly, 'and they were frightened.'

Not Norman, I thought. Not the fat man, transformed and self-intoxicated. But Bernard might have been. Not frightened – that wasn't his style – but cautious.

A different question occurred to me. 'Can you get to the pool from the road?' The day I walked up to the croft on the hill I hadn't seen a track off to the left, but there was no reason why I should have noticed one.

Without answering, she stepped away to fade back in the darkness.

When I went inside, Eileen was in the same place, hands

clasped in front of her on the table. I sat down beside her and, after a moment, put my hand on hers. It was the first time I had touched her in a way that made a claim upon her. She didn't move her hands from under mine.

'Are you sorry?' she asked.

'I'm sorry,' I said. I thought she meant for going off and leaving her behind.

'For running away with me?'

'I never meant to get you into so much trouble,' I said.

'I'm not sorry I met you. I'm selfish enough not to be sorry for that.'

'I wouldn't change anything.' The clumsy words were all I could find.

'My life had stopped,' she said, 'and now it's begun again. Whatever happens.'

We sat for a long time. We didn't talk again. We were shy with one another. The light from the lamp on the table grew dim; perhaps the wick needed to be trimmed or the oil was low. The plates and glasses sat in pools of shadow. Once I heard her sigh and I tightened my hand on hers. I'd rowed at the seaside, but I'd never experienced what I'd seen once in a film: a man and woman carried in a boat on a calm river, his oars hardly feathering the water. Among the shadows, we were drifting and I had no thoughts I could put into words. At last, something, perhaps a night bird crying or the easing of peats in the grate, brought me back to my senses. I thought of Bernard and wondered if the two of us should simply set out across the fields before he came back, run off into the darkness and hope it would hide us. At that moment I heard the murmur of voices outside.

I had the momentary impulse to take my hand from Eileen's, even to retreat to the other side of the table. When she made no movement, I found the courage to sit still.

It was Beate, however, who appeared in the doorway. She stood looking at us for a moment in silence, then she turned away and we heard her feet on the bare treads as she went upstairs.

'I thought she'd gone to bed,' Eileen said softly.

I shook my head, not wanting to speak in case my voice trembled.

'How much longer?' she asked.

Like me, she was thinking of Bernard, his malice and what it might make him do.

The agony was prolonged. It was August who finally arrived. Like his sister, he stood watching us from the doorway.

'You waited up,' he said. 'That was thoughtful of you.'

When I heard the note of mockery in his voice, I knew that something had happened.

'Is my husband with you?' Eileen asked.

He shook his head. 'I walked back,' he said. I realised there had been no sound of a car. 'That's what took the time.'

'Back from the pond?' I asked.

He ignored me. His eyes never left Eileen; I might not have spoken.

'They put the case in the car and off they went,' he told her.

No sound of a car. Could I have missed it going past on the road outside?

'All the way back, I thought they'd be here before me. But it looks,' he said to her, 'as if your husband got what he came for and left.'

'Yes,' she said. Her voice wasn't much more than a whisper. Next day, I would try to understand how much damage these last years must have done to her self-esteem. At that moment, though, I waited in panic for her to protest that she didn't believe him. Instead she looked at me and half whispered in the same gentle, withdrawn voice, 'I think I'll go to bed now, if you don't mind.'

He hardly stood aside for her, so that she had to push past him.

When she had gone, he said, 'Why don't you go upstairs and join her?'

His words startled me like a threat. He smiled as if I amused him. 'Why shouldn't you sleep with her?' he asked. 'She isn't your mother.'

The brutality of it stunned me. If he didn't respect Eileen, what chance did we have?

Alone, I listened for a third time to steps mounting the bare stairway and the gentle percussion of a closing door.

CHAPTER THIRTY-NINE

When Beate came down in the morning, I had lain awake all night and was tired to the bone. I listened to her making the usual morning sounds and lay without stirring. I had a child's impulse to pull the covers over my head and shut out the world.

After a time, I was surprised to feel a hand on my shoulder.

When I sat up, she was holding out a bowl of porridge with the spoon sitting in it.

'No.' She pressed me back when I went to get up. 'Sup it where you are. And the tea's made, and there's an egg, if you want one.'

I muttered some sort of thanks. To add to my discomfort she sat at the end of the couch and there was nothing for it but to stir the spoon in the bowl and begin.

'I took a tray up to Eileen,' she said.

'I'll finish this and get up.'

'When I was a child, I loved my breakfast in bed.'

I couldn't think of anything to say to that.

'What about you?' she asked.

I was ashamed to tell her I couldn't remember ever being given breakfast in bed.

'Maybe you were never ill,' she said, as if she had read my thoughts. 'I got it in my bed when I had a cold. A bit ill, but not too much, was best.'

She was using again that oddly colourless accent both of them had used in the beginning – so that it had been possible to believe they were from South Africa, since their voices carried no claim to belonging anywhere.

'I sometimes thought it would be nice to get it for no reason – I mean, not have to be ill at all. But even if such a thought had occurred to my mother, my father would never have allowed it. Would your father?'

I was cramming the porridge in, but the bowl was full to overflowing and it took time. Swallowing in a gulp, I mumbled, 'He wouldn't have minded.'

She put her head to one side regarding me thoughtfully. When she walked, she stooped a little, trying perhaps to make herself smaller, and that went with a certain clumsiness in the way she walked. Sitting there, however, busy with her own thoughts, she was unselfconsciously erect and graceful. Sitting in half-profile, too, her round features, which could look placid, even stupid at times, sharpened and took on character so that she seemed almost handsome. Normally pale, she had a spot of red on each cheek.

'He sounds nice, your father. Is he?'

'I suppose so.'

'You don't sound very sure.'

I didn't feel like explaining that he was dead.

'He's all right,' I said.

'So he's still alive?'

'Yes!' The single word came out more abruptly than I'd intended. I was afraid and tired, and there was a repressed excitement about her which disturbed me.

If I had spoken sharply, she seemed to pay no attention. 'What about your mother?' she asked. When I hesitated, she went on, 'Your real one, I mean.'

Of course, that deception was over.

'She's alive,' I said.

I had to pull up my feet to avoid brushing against her as I swung my legs out from under the blanket. As I put the empty bowl on the table, Beate lifted the pillow and began to fold the blanket, patting the heavy folds. I put on my trousers, not turning away from her, since I didn't feel like a boy any more, modest or not.

'Give me a minute,' she said, 'and I'll get your egg.'

'No, don't bother.'

'It isn't any bother.'

'But I'm not fussed. If it's all right, I could cut myself some bread and cheese. I'd prefer that, honestly.'

'Oh, well, if you won't let me spoil you. That's what my father called it, "spoiling". Sometimes August spoils me. But don't say I told you. He wouldn't be pleased.'

Eileen came down, dressed and carrying her tray, as I was eating at the table.

'How are you feeling?' Beate asked.

'I'm all right. I'm not ill any more. You really shouldn't have bothered.'

'It isn't any bother,' she said again. 'I wish I could make the two of you believe that. I'm happy to do things for you.' The spots of red glowed on her cheeks. 'After the excitement, a little spoiling does no harm. I gave this one his porridge in bed, but he wouldn't stay for the rest. You know what men are like.' She sounded almost skittish, not heavy or grave as she had before. She was turning into someone different, but then what did I know about who she really was?

Eileen avoided my eye as she put the tray on the table, and went out without another word.

'Oh, dear,' Beate said, looking after her. 'That's the first morning she hasn't offered to help with the washing up. Perhaps she isn't as well as she thinks.'

'I'll do it.'

I began to lift the cup, plate and cutlery from the tray.

'No.' She stopped me. 'Go and talk to her. I'm sure you must want to.'

I found Eileen just inside the gate to the road, looking with folded arms in the direction the brothers would have taken to begin their homeward journey the previous evening. Though the gate was open, I had the odd impression of her being held behind an obstruction that barred her way. She gave no sign as I came to her side.

'Are you all right?' I asked.

'After the excitement, you mean?' She stared out at the road. 'Isn't that what that awful woman called it?'

Inanely I said, 'I thought you liked her.'

'Can't you see she's laughing at us?'

I started to answer but stopped, unsure of the truth.

'I opened my eyes and she was looking down at me. I'm sure she hadn't knocked, just walked in. All I wanted was a chance to be quiet and think. The last thing I wanted was breakfast.'

'She did that to me, too,' I said. 'But I was awake. I couldn't sleep all night.'

We stood together, penned behind the invisible barrier.

'What was in the case?' she asked.

I told her.

'A lot of money?'

'A fortune.'

'So that's what it was about.' She was quiet for a moment, lost in thought, and then she astonished me. 'Mr Gas: isn't that what Bernard called you? That's what he's like. Once I told him our neighbour was going to be sixty, and next day I heard him say, "I hear you're having a birthday? Fifty, is it?" And he smiled when the man didn't deny it. He probes for weakness. Even with me. Right from the beginning. Even when he loved me.'

As she said that, it was suddenly clear to me how little I believed the money was what Bernard cared about.

'Perhaps he still does,' I said on an impulse I regretted at once.

She looked at me with a kind of dismay that turned to anger.

'There comes a time when that doesn't matter,' she said. 'Even a woman can learn that love doesn't excuse everything.' And then, while I hesitated, she asked, 'And if he does, why didn't he come back?'

I took her by the arm. 'We could go right now. Just go out on to the road and start walking.'

She shook her head. 'I feel drained of energy. But if you want to walk, why don't you go by yourself?'

'I don't mean for a walk. I mean, leave – get away from here.'

'Could we?' She spoke as if the breath had been driven from her body. 'We're miles from anywhere.'

Before I could put into words what I had lived with, shapeless and horrible, like an unfocused shadow on the edge of thought, August called my name. From no direction, it seemed to come from the air. For the first time in my life, I felt my heart beat so strangely it felt it might shake itself from my chest.

He was in shadow between the open doors of the barn. 'It's a job that takes two,' he said. He wanted me to help him cut out and replace rotted beams. 'The new wood came when you were away. It's needed fixing for a long time.'

We worked together all morning, as we had done several times before. It was heavy work and my shoulders ached after an hour of it, but he seemed tireless and pride or fear kept me going, matching him hour after hour. Several times it struck me how carefully, even regretfully, he lifted aside the birds' nests that were tucked into the angles of the old beams. Towards the end, with the pace he set and my tiredness, I had to keep wiping sweat from my eyes. When at last he stopped and went out, I sat with my back against one of the stalls, drawing in breaths thick enough to chew of the still, heavy air.

All too soon he was back, carrying a jug of tea and sandwiches. 'No point in stopping too long. It'll take us the rest of the day, maybe tomorrow as well.' Most of the morning he'd said nothing, now he offered occasional sentences, thrown out like scraps of the food he was masticating. 'If I was ever able to travel, this place would need to be in shape for selling.'

He shook the last of the tea on to the ground and went out again. I stood in the doorway and watched him cross the yard. As soon as I saw him go into the outside toilet on the end wall of the house, I realised that was where I needed to go, too. After ten minutes, the need was so urgent that I went over and waited for him to be finished.

When August opened the door at last, though, he didn't come out but stood blocking the entrance.

He smiled at me and said, 'I was thinking while I was sitting in there about the priest on Barra. It must have been the smell of shit that put him in my head. This child I was fond of – she was like a sister to me – wasn't well. It was his belief that he had the power to cast out evil spirits. According to him, there was nothing for it but an exorcism. Her parents had too much of the peasant in them to argue with a priest. But I hid myself and watched, wanting to take care of her. Do you know anything about such things? Not many people do. I read up on it, but that was when I had the chance and it was years later. As far as I remember, he went through the whole rigmarole, but there were no turds, not even a wet fart, in fact. And she didn't speak in tongues, not a word. It is possible, of course, that the Devil wasn't in her, after all. Would you think that might be it? Oh, I have to tell you it was a disappointment. Between you and me, I'd put great hopes in it. And will I tell you what was the worst thing? The wee man had a pimple on the side of his nose, and looking in the window it surprised me to see the pimple still there. I wondered afterwards if it was me seeing the pimple meant the girl was left in the power of the Devil.'

When he stood aside, I went in at a rush and sat down and braced my foot against the door – there was no lock. But at once I stood again, as if pushed up by the stink from the bowl. Through a crack in the planks, I watched August cross the yard and go into the byre, and when he was out of sight I opened the door and simply walked out of the gate and kept going.

CHAPTER FORTY

I had acted by instinct and found myself on the road with no
plan. I was walking in the direction I'd taken the day I met the
crofter, and with that thought it occurred to me I could go to
him for help. He had warned me against August and, though old,
he had seemed fearless. If he would come back with me; if he
would give us a run to the nearest town . . . It might be a lot to
ask, but what else was there to do? I looked for him in the field
where I'd first seen him, but the cows mooched across it
undisturbed. Under the full weight of the sun, the air between
the hedges clung to me like a burden. I could hear a bird's double
note, faint and persistent, and the buzz of insects in the grass.
There was no song, however, no music blaring from a wireless,
no sign of life from the house on top of the hill.

I told myself it was a warm day, but reasonably or not it
bothered me that there was no smoke from the chimneys. As I
got closer, I couldn't hear any voices or stir of movement. Unlike
where I'd come from, the area in front of the house was a kind of
junkyard littered with old pieces of equipment. A dark stain of oil
showed where a car had been parked, but the space was empty.
With a sinking heart, I knocked, then banged, on the door. I
turned the handle and it opened, but I knew that meant nothing.
If they were away on an errand, it wouldn't occur to them to lock
up before they left. It was the same layout as August's place. The
kitchen was dark and crammed with ancient furniture. A faint
smell of stale cooking hung on the air. I called up the stairs and,
met by silence, tried again more loudly. I had no heart for a third
time.

Between one moment and the next, the suppressed desire to
shit reasserted itself. I searched for the toilet with the urgency of a
fire engine in an emergency. By the time I found it, tucked away

at the far end of the house, lights were spinning and the siren was wailing. It was only with the luxury of relief that it occurred to me how embarrassing it would have been if the old folk had, in fact, been around. To make sure, I walked out of the yard on the side opposite the road. Luckily there were no horned cattle in that field, and I walked down the slope to the edge of the water. It stretched out of sight to the left, but wasn't all that wide ahead of me, not more than a mile across.

I watched the progress of a pair of swans across the middle of the little loch. On the near side, brown birds I took to be ducks took turns tipping upside down to stick their heads underwater. The bank dropped to a cuticle of sand on which a boat was drawn up out of the water. Two oars lay tidily in the bottom. On impulse, I stepped in and sat down. Just as I did, an engine sounded across the quiet water. Like a man on a desert island, I jumped up at once and waved my arms, but the car passed left to right along the far side and vanished.

I sat in the boat for a long time and left it reluctantly. It was strange. When I'd run off before, I'd had no hesitation in going to find the Morton brothers and returning with them. It had never occurred to me not to come back, and that was before I was in love with Eileen, or at least knew I was. Now, despite knowing, there was a terrible temptation to push the boat into the water and escape. The difference between then and now was a measure of the change I had come to feel in the presence of August. I had no protection now of doubt or scepticism. It would have been easy to give in to my desire for escape. What stopped me from pushing the boat into the water was not my love for Eileen but the extraordinary fact of her love for me.

I couldn't face going back to the road. Instead, I turned my back on the loch and walked to where the field ended in bushes and a line of trees. I wound through them till I was stopped by a languid stream, too dark to be shallow and too wide to jump. There came a place, though, where after winding back and forward the water gathered pace to cut a narrower channel, and just after this rocks acted as stepping stones to the other side. The footing was wet, slimy in parts, and when the last rock wobbled under my weight it took an awkward lunge to make the bank. The tangle of bushes came close to the water's edge, but there was the faint trace of an almost overgrown path and I made reasonable speed until a fallen tree blocked my way. If there had been any choice, I would have turned back but I put my arms across my face and scrambled through a mass of branches and then inched through, bent double, where the fallen trunk rested on the broken base. As soon as I was on the other side the path was wider, and another dozen steps took me to a place I recognised. It was the pool where Eileen and I had eaten Beate's picnic; in another life, it seemed.

Despite the rocks scattered around, it was a pleasant place to sit. There were no trees in the corner of the field on the other side; and the sun, lower in the sky, slanted across on to the grass. Anyway, most of the rocks by the pool were small. There weren't more than half a dozen larger ones. I went from one to the other and turned them over. The biggest one I left to the end. It took two hands and bent knees to tip it over. There was no hole underneath, nor traces of earth removed to make a hiding place for a case full of money. I sat down beside it and stared across the water, my head so full of my own thoughts that it was some time before I noticed the marks.

A pair of parallel lines ran from top to bottom of the opposite bank, just missing a narrow patch of sand, and disappeared at the water's edge. No more than scuff marks in the grass, they were very faint. The next shower of rain would rub them away; the marks of a car's tyres. If I'd sat to one side or the other, I might well not have seen them. When I stood, I lost them; and turned instead to staring down into the water.

I could see nothing, but at the thought of going in I remembered how deep the pool had been and the soft, clutching mud that had let me go so reluctantly.

CHAPTER FORTY-ONE

I stepped softly as I went back into the yard, but August's voice reached out from the barn and caught me. To my surprise, he didn't ask where I'd been, but got me started working again, and another couple of hours went by in a sweat of physical labour. By the time Eileen appeared to announce the meal was ready, I was on the verge of exhaustion. Looking as fresh as he had in the morning, August jumped down and went over to the house. More slowly, I came down the ladder, calling to her to wait for me.

'I've something to tell you.'

We stood close together just inside the door of the barn. I searched for words that wouldn't come. Emotion, lack of sleep, physical weariness, muddled my thoughts. 'We can't be too long,' I said three or four times, and the need to hurry only made things harder. Somehow I got it said. My hoarse whisper claiming Norman and Bernard were dead carried no conviction, though, even to my own ears. When I stumbled to an end, I saw not just disbelief in her face, but alarm and something like pity.

We went across the yard in silence.

As I sat down, I saw Eileen look behind me. In the same instant, August put his hands on my shoulders. I twisted round and looked up at him.

'Look upon this Thy servant Harry,' he intoned solemnly as he held me, 'who is grievously vexed with the wiles of an unclean spirit, whom the old adversary, the ancient enemy of the earth, encompasses with dread.'

The hairs rose on the back of my neck.

'You should see the look on your face!' Beate said to me.

Infected by her laughter, August began to chuckle. Sitting down opposite Eileen, he said, 'I was telling Harry I once saw a priest doing an exorcism. That was part of it.'

'Did it work?' Eileen asked unsmilingly.

'He had a pimple on his nose,' August said, and he and Beate began laughing again.

It was like a party to which neither Eileen nor I had been invited.

August heaped his fork with potato and fat bacon and spoke with his mouth full. 'I read up on that stuff in a book. You can find anything if you know where to look,' he said. 'I could have done Honours at the university, but I took an ordinary degree and got out.'

'Do you regret that?' Eileen asked.

He glanced at her and said, 'Don't be stupid.'

It was brutal and casual. At the opposite end of the table from Beate, I caught the glance she gave Eileen. Avid and expectant, her glance, as much as the man's words, appalled me.

Eileen seemed utterly taken aback. When she spoke, however, her voice was calm and she held his gaze steadily. 'Why would that be stupid?'

'Books you find for yourself are what count. That's how a man learns what matters.'

'Do you believe that, too?'

Seeking an ally, she turned to Beate, who offered a smile, modest, almost tentative. I had left Eileen undefended. I had found the courage to tell her August might be a murderer, but the matter of incest had stuck in my throat.

'Did she tell you she was a reader? If you want the truth,' he said, and I felt my heart contract, 'that woman there – what's the best way to put it? – you could say she makes things up.'

'We've all been guilty of that.' Eileen looked from one to the other. Her tone was interested but almost casual, determinedly clinging to some notion of normality. 'I know I have. I suppose you have, too.'

He forked in another giant mouthful and, without taking his eyes from her, chewed it open-mouthed, with greedy relish. I couldn't take my eyes from him. He had never eaten like that in front of us. If before he had been putting on a show, he had taken off the mask. If he hadn't, what point was he making? He got the last of it down before he spoke.

'Have you ever heard of Havelock Ellis?'

'What a strange name,' Eileen said. It was as if, having nothing else, she was drawing on some reserve of social skills or habit.

'Not at all. Nothing *foreign* about it,' he said. 'My foot is on my native heath, and my name is Havelock. Which doesn't mean he wasn't a bloody fool. He built a whole theory of female psychology on the fact his mother once peed in front of him when he was a small boy. They wore long skirts in those days and he heard it hissing down into the grass. It never occurred to him she might have needed to pee so badly that it didn't matter he was there. What do you think? I mean, as a *mother.*'

A strange thing happened then, for I looked at Eileen and knew her thoughts. At that moment, we were one flesh. The horrible part of it was that what I understood was that she had lost all her scepticism. She knew that Bernard and Norman were dead.

'I wasn't a mother for very long,' she said.

Brother and sister looked at me, then at one another, and grinned. It wasn't a smile, but a grin, empty-hearted and stupid.

'I had a daughter,' Eileen said, 'but she died.'

The grin faded, not at once but slowly, as if they were reluctant to let it go. If I had been stronger, I would have upended the table on them. But I wasn't grown into my full strength and he was stronger than most men. If I'd been wiser or better or braver, I might have found words to defend her. But he was the one who had read all the books.

'Death is a thing you never get to the end of considering,' he said. 'It comes in so many ways. It's always terrible in a child, but it can be peaceful in an old man. Not that my father's death was peaceful. We were all exhausted, and I made the women go to bed and I sat through the night with him. I watched as he fought for every breath, fought till the last one he drew, and all my love for him made no difference.' His eyes gleamed as if about to fill with tears. 'I'll tell you something silly. He said once that washing your hair too often weakened it. Not even speaking to me, something I overheard, and thinking of it now I suppose he must have been joking. Yet it's influenced me all my life – not that my hair's dirty, but certainly I don't wash it often.'

'I'm glad I wasn't there when my father died,' Eileen said, 'but I didn't love him.'

Her words took him by surprise, for he blinked and lost his thread.

'Too soft-hearted,' Beate said. She was staring from her end of the table, and for a moment I thought she was referring to me. 'The morning of the day these two came here, there was a pigeon the cat had caught. It had a wing torn off. But you couldn't kill it. I told you it had to be done. But it was me that wrung its neck.'

'Sometimes a thing hits you the wrong way,' he said.

'But you admit—'

'Oh, it had to be done.'

'And if a thing like that happened again?'

'Something that had to be done?'

'You wouldn't leave it to me again?'

'Next time,' August said, 'I'd take care of it.'

There was a silence no one filled. I ate with my eyes on my plate, putting the food in my mouth without tasting it. When the plates were empty, they were tidied away. Some nights, after the main course there had been cheese and tea, but there was no offer of them tonight. He talked of the long day and how tired I looked; and so I was made the reason for Eileen having to go to bed, separated again from me. Before she left, he said to her, 'In the dark night of the soul it is always three in the morning. I read that somewhere. Death's only one of the things that can make us grieve.'

I don't know if it was three o'clock, but it was dark when I wakened. I couldn't believe I'd slept. I'd lain down in fear and dropped off the moment I closed my eyes. I listened to myself panting, and wondered why my breath was coming so quickly. Then I heard it. Someone was coming down the stairs. As the footsteps came into the hall outside the open door, I closed my eyes and lay still. For certain, someone stood over me, but it was only a change in the air that told me so. Then there was nothing for a moment and after that I heard a second person coming down. The agonising pause of expectation ended with the distinctive grating sound of the front door being drawn open and afterwards pulled shut.

I got up and dressed, and went upstairs carrying my shoes in my hand. If we were to be saved, this was our chance. I didn't think about that, I just knew that escape would be achieved quickly or not at all.

When I opened the bedroom door, I heard her take a breath and understood that she must have been lying awake.

'They've gone for a walk,' I whispered.

'In the middle of the night?'

'If we're ever to get away, we have to do it now.'

While she dressed, I told her my plan. Provided we could get out of the gate unseen, we could follow the road as I had done the day before. If the crofter and his wife were at home, we could seek help. If they weren't, we would try to cross the loch in the boat. It was a poor plan, but I could think of nothing else. It seemed to me our only chance.

Eileen, however, had been doing her own thinking in those hours she lay awake in the dark. I was faced with the result at once; the reasons for it I worked out later. She blamed herself that we had stolen the case from her husband. If he had been killed for its contents, his death was her fault and there was no way in the world she would accept it being left with August. Moreover, she knew the case was not under a rock by the pool, for I had told her so. That being so, the likeliest thing was for him to have concealed it in the house.

When, over my protests, she opened the door of their bedroom, we saw the smallest circle of light imaginable thrown on the floor from a little guttering candle acting as a night-light. One of them – Beate, I suppose – must have had trouble sleeping without it.

There are different kinds of courage. When I whispered that I would go and keep guard, I sold it to myself as a sensible precaution. The truth was it took more nerve than I had to stay and watch her search, and I had even less stomach for helping her.

When I peeped out into the yard, my heart sank. From the half-open door of the shed beside the barn, light spilled across the gateway like a barrier to block our escape.

I went back up the stairs and into the bedroom. I must have held my breath all the way, for I had to let the air sigh out of me before I could tell her, 'They're in the shed.'

'Must we go now?' she asked.

'If we can.'

The wardrobe doors were open and she had pulled out drawers and must have moved the bed to look under it, for the sheets had slid off and shaped a crouching in the candlelight. She shook her head, accepting that we had to go, but held out her hands in despair to show me they were empty.

I had taken a step out of the doorway, when I realised what I had seen. I watched Eileen going down the stairs, and ached to follow her but turned back instead. As I went back into the room, I hoped that I had been mistaken. But it was there above the wardrobe, the shadowy shape of the case's handle where it leaned against the wall. I was only just able to see it; Eileen wasn't tall enough. It was right at the back, forcing me to get on tiptoe and stretch. An awkward clutch knocked it to the side. For a second, until it stuck, I thought it was going to fall all the way. The wardrobe was solid, maybe too much for me to move on my own. I couldn't see the handle now, only feel it, and I hadn't enough leverage to pull it up from where it was caught. In my terror, I wanted to give up. My heart thundered as if it would burst, but the heart is a tough muscle when you are young. I pulled over the little chest of drawers and scrambled up on to it. Next moment I had the case and was back on the stairs, rushing to get out into the open air.

When I saw Eileen standing by the door of the shed beside the barn, I felt a surge of rage at the folly of it that was almost hatred for her. There is no rage like the rage of fear. Taking care to keep out of the path of light that flowed from the open door, I crossed the yard to her, step by cautious step. Between the jamb and the door, there was a gap through which I peered into a space lit by one lamp set down in the doorway, throwing most of its light out into the yard, and another hanging from a hook above a bench.

It was the interior in which I'd seen a bound thing struggling for life.

Afterwards, I could never be sure of what I glimpsed, whether or not there was a figure on the bench and whether another crouched over it. Eileen took me by the shoulder and pushed me aside. I might have resisted or tried to draw her away, but let her hold me like that so that I could not see. The scar of narrow light drew itself like a blade down her face.

Out of the stillness and the darkness, I heard a whisper, intimate, anonymous, yet unmistakably the voice of August.

'How will I start?'

'Put me out of all this pain.'

'A little breast meat,' he said, 'that's always the sweetest.'

I had witnessed him kill a pig by cutting its throat, and I imagined the same knife in his hand, blade sharpened to an edge like a razor's. I had no doubt she was about to die.

'Do it. Stop tormenting me.'

'Put your head back for me.'

At the pressure of Eileen's hand on my shoulder, I almost screamed aloud. She pushed me ahead of her and we moved like that to the far end of the yard and half a dozen steps along the river path before I made myself stop.

'We can't do this.'

'Come *on*!'

'He's killing her.'

'No, he's not.'

'I heard him.'

'Heard? What did you hear? He's lying on top of her and she's in such a frenzy she's lifting the weight of him in the air. Isn't that what you heard?'

'They're making love?'

'Call it that,' she said. 'Let that be enough. Please.'

It was too dark under the trees to see her face.

If I allowed myself to be drawn forward, though I knew in my heart that one day he would kill her and that day would be the end of him, it was because I had a vision of her white face at table, eyes fixed on him with the gaze of a hypnotist, and could not tell which of them dreamed the nightmare in which they lived.

CHAPTER FORTY-TWO

The mist made it an act of faith for Eileen to set out on the loch with me. We could see no more than a hundred yards to where it stood up out of the water like a white wall. I, at least, had seen the far shore and knew it was within reach. I didn't have to take it on trust. As far as she could tell, we might have been on the shore of the sea itself.

The first few strokes, desperate to hurry, I tried too hard. I smacked the surface and scooped so awkwardly I fell backwards. After that, I found some rhythm and we began to cut through the water. Even when we went into the mist, I kept up the same pace, concentrating on the dip and pull until, not slowly but suddenly, the oars became like leaden weights that I could hardly lift.

'Is it much further?' Her face was only a shape of whiteness. The words might have been spoken by the mist itself.

With a groan I bent forwards, staring at my hands. They were locked into claws, the backs beaded with blood where I had pushed aside branches under the fallen tree after we had drawn one another past the pool, its surface dark and shiny as the lid of a coffin. Resolved to get through and find the line of rocks to cross the stream, I hadn't felt the stabbing of the thorns as they dug into me.

'It wasn't this far,' I said.

'But it's hard to tell, when we can't see.'

'We should be at the other side.'

'There's nothing to guide you.'

'I could be rowing down the loch. Or in circles.'

I heard panic rise like floodwater, scummed and swirling, under my words. I had lost us. I could do nothing right. I would steer back at last to a bank where a naked woman and a man waited for us, the man with a knife in his hand.

'It's not your fault,' the mist voice said.

In response, I lifted the oars again and the sound of them striking the water was answered. From somewhere ahead of us, an engine coughed into life.

It was a lorry pulled into a passing place on the single-lane road. The driver had been wakened by the cold and started the engine to warm the cabin. He gave us a lift all the way to Aberdeen, and didn't ask any questions, being more interested in his life than ours. The parliament in London, apparently, had just passed a law that would make separation for seven years grounds for a divorce. The question was, would it apply in Scotland, which had its own legal system? He and his wife had been parted for three years. 'Only four to go,' he explained more than once. He wouldn't take any money and in the depot in Aberdeen found another lorry for us. That was how we got as far as Manchester. That driver took money from Eileen, and she had only enough left in her purse to pay for one room for a night in the cheapest boarding house we could find. In the room, she put down the small case from August's bedroom. Once we'd found it, she'd shown no interest in the contents and I decided discussing what we should do could wait till morning.

A faint smell of stale smoke hung in the air. A cigarette stub sat in a tin ashtray on the night table by the bed. Apart from the bed, there was a single chair by the window, a wardrobe, a folding canvas stand to take a case, a hanging bulb with a brown shade, and in a corner a lamp which flickered and went out when we tried it. It was a double bed.

She began to take her clothes off and I pulled my shirt over my head. We hadn't kissed or touched one another. We undressed standing on either side of the bed, and when I was stripped I stood and watched as she became naked. I saw the hair between her legs and the weight of her breasts, the way they were big and hung down a little. She knelt on the bed, and leaning on it with one hand reached and took hold of me. I felt her hand close round me and by some miracle I didn't explode. She lay on her back and drew me on top of her. When I felt myself go in, I cried, 'I'm in, oh, I'm in!' and she tightened on me and then it happened. I tensed when I heard her laughing, and then I realised she was laughing not at me but with me, and what was between us was sealed and sealed for ever. And then she came over on top of me.

It was like passing out the way I went to sleep, but when I woke up she was still there. I eased my arm out from under her and got up and put out the light. Even when I'd done that, the room wasn't really dark for there was a lamp in the corridor kept on all night, perhaps in case anyone sneaked off without paying, and light leaked in under the door.

From the bed, her voice whispered, 'Would they have killed us?'

'Oh, I think so,' I said.

I got back in and she turned towards me and I put my hand between her legs and she opened up and that was the second time. The second time she started to move, suddenly heaving her body up, lifting me, grinding against me. She shook and groaned and even when she stopped I went on, back and forward, and she came again and this time I did, too. This time I didn't go to sleep. I wasn't sure whether she was awake. She didn't say anything. I wanted to see her face, but it was tucked against my shoulder. I lay in the dark and listened to her breathing, and at some point I must have fallen asleep for she wasn't beside me. I sat up in a panic, and an indrawn breath made me see her, in the chair near the window.

I got out of bed and pulled up the blinds. It was early. A little sun glowed like a cinder through a bolster of clouds bunched over the slate roofs of the buildings.

'I'm all right,' she said. 'It isn't cold.'

'Why did you get up?' And when she didn't answer, 'What are you thinking about?'

'It isn't interesting.'

'Tell me.'

'You asked me why I married. Do you remember? If I was so happy as a nurse, you said, so glad to be free of my father. I waited for you to ask me if it was because Bernard was rich.' I made an inarticulate noise mixing protest and apology. 'It's true those last months on my own were the happiest of my life. The week before our wedding I went to Bernard's house to tell him I didn't want to go through with it. He said to me, "You don't know what you want." He didn't raise his voice, but for the first time – wasn't I a fool? – I understood how terrible it would be for him, in front of all his friends – he had so much pride. I can't remember what I said. I was trying to say how sorry I was for him. I think it was my pity that made him rape me. At first I tried to stop him, but he went on. He went on until I didn't want to stop him. At one point as I climaxed, I cried out, and he said, "Quietly! My father's upstairs." After that, I didn't try to resist marrying any more. All night I didn't want to stop him.'

Not finding words, I held her in the circle of my arms. Enfolding her, I made a bargain with myself that I would do everything I could to stop her going to the police. What justice could there be in anything that might separate us? One of the Morton brothers a murderer, the other a rapist: the world was better off without them. August and Beate were their own punishment. The police might not believe us. I had all the arguments. Yet even then, bending into the mingled scent of our lovemaking to kiss her, I knew that every bargain has its price.

In a dry tone almost of disbelief she whispered, 'And now he's dead. What are we going to do?'

'Live,' I said.

When we went out in the morning, I didn't check the number or the name of the street, for it was just a cheap boarding house lost in an anonymous wilderness of red brick in one or another suburb of the city we stopped in for a night on our way to London.

EPILOGUE

Beginnings

CHAPTER FORTY-THREE

The cardiologist didn't ask about Eileen, so I'd no chance to tell him we'd lived together for over fifty years and that she was dead and what was wrong with my heart was that it was broken. That would have embarrassed both of us. My GP had offered the consolation that she was very old, and I hadn't told him how little that mattered. If she had been a hundred, something in me would have cried out in anger against her death.

It wasn't true that we never quarrelled, yet I think of our worst quarrel as happiness, since I was with her. Apart from our first time together, Eileen used a diaphragm – a Dutch cap, they called it then – when we made love. Maybe she felt I was too young for the responsibility of children; maybe, at first, she imagined I might leave if she were pregnant. Afterwards, when she stopped, I used condoms until one day she asked me why. I told her that the doctor said it would be dangerous if she had a baby. 'At my age?' she wondered bitterly. That's how it was at that time. In later years I couldn't bear to hear of those mothers of forty or more, even mothers of fifty! And when she told me, "I'd risk dying for your child," it was too late – it never happened.

I'd been nodding wherever it seemed appropriate as the cardiologist talked, but now I realised he'd fallen silent and was looking at me. 'You're taking this very calmly,' he said. 'Are you sure you understand what I'm saying?'

My mother was dead. My father had died long ago. My wife was dead. I had met her in the middle of the last century. It was just before the British had herded the Kikuyu together, when men's mouths were filled with mud and some were beaten to death in a camp called Hola. Were preparations undertaken that year, contracts made, bribes taken? What did it matter? After the

Nazi death camps, all of us knew that Europe of the high culture was a continent of torturers. That was the dirty secret of the dull Fifties and all the decades that followed. What did it matter? The sickness was in the air and it travelled to all the continents of the world so that it seemed colour and creed no longer mattered since they were only excuses for what united men, their need to hurt one another. What did it matter? After beating away unnoticed all my life, my heart had turned traitor. In the republic of the body, it had grown restless. It was a presence now, a dull space, a hollowness or a tremor that left me feeling squeamish.

It seemed that I had come to a destination out of the corner of my eye as it were, for when I got up at three in the morning, after lying awake for hours, I found not one but three unopened containers of opiates in the medicine cabinet. I shaved, avoiding my eyes in the mirror, dressed more carefully than usual, and took the pills down to the kitchen.

I had them piled high in front of a bottle of whisky and the first glass poured when I thought that someone would have to find me. I shrank from the idea of a neighbour alarmed by a smell; a workman coming on me by accident. I would write a letter to the police, I decided, and go out now and post it. Deep in thought, the chime of the doorbell startled me to my feet. I peered cautiously through the glass of the front door, and made out a shape darker than the night behind it. For an instant I believed it was the police, and was as bewildered as if I were already dead.

I was astonished to find my neighbour on the step. He had been with one of the banks, working on acquisitions, but had already retired when we took the house next to them. He was fully dressed, with his coat on, and carrying a plastic shopping bag.

'Walter?' I asked, as if testing an improbability.

'I saw your kitchen light was on. Can I come in?'

I stepped aside but then, as he headed down the corridor, remembered the pills and whisky and directed him into the front room. Unlike the kitchen, the front of the house faced north and the leather of the armchair felt cold as we settled on either side of the empty hearth.

We were neighbours, not friends. We chatted across the garden fence in summer. 'I flew all over Europe on business. Enjoyed every minute of it. I won't tell you I don't miss it. I feel I could still do it, but nowadays it's all about what age you are. And it wasn't all business. What people don't know doesn't hurt them, and I wouldn't have hurt Jean for the world, but when you're far from home, eh? You know what they say: on your deathbed, it's not the women you've slept with you'll regret, it's the ones you haven't!' How many times I'd heard Walter on that refrain, like a continuous loop. It alternated with an interest in maps and military campaigns, fuelled, it seemed, by nostalgia for national service. When I told him I'd missed out on those delights because of flat feet, I'd gone down in his estimation.

That was Walter, thick glasses, round belly, white hair, soldier and Casanova. Eileen had liked Jean, who had welcomed us when we moved in and died the following year of cancer of the stomach. That was something we had now in common, being widowers, but this was only the second time Walter had been in my front room.

His previous visit had been a strange one, too. 'I don't know if you'll even feel like voting. Your wife not long taken from you, but life goes on, I found that.' I'd had a strong temptation to take him by the neck and throw him over the doorstep, but had brought him in here instead; welcoming him as a voice to break the silence. 'I've never done this before, Harry, going round the doors like this. It's a new party – just a small one, but it'll grow, I shouldn't be surprised, and I think you're exactly the kind of man it'll appeal to.' As he rhymed off policies on education, health and fishing, it made a kind of sense, though all slightly askew, like politics conducted through the looking glass. 'And then there's the constitution. What we're going to do is get rid of the MEPs and reduce the number of MPs from seventy-two to fifty-six. And they'll do both jobs, Holyrood and Westminster. That way, you see, we'll be able to get rid of the new parliament building and all the MSPs as well, and there'll be no problem about reserved powers.' At that point, I'd started to laugh; but he, it seemed, was perfectly serious and he'd left a leaflet as proof.

Now, settling down opposite me, he declared, 'It's like a sign, finding you up at this hour and still dressed.'

'I was reading.'

'I do that, fall asleep over the book. You're tired but you can't face going to bed.'

We looked at each other in silence.

'Thing is,' Walter said eventually, 'I've got a sister lives in Castlemilk. Respectable woman, but life hasn't been easy for her. The scheme's gone down since she first got a council house there.'

'Yes?' Just the one cautious word. It was possible the man was a secret drinker.

'I visited her a month ago, and when I came out someone had scratched the Jaguar. A key or some bloody thing right along the side of it. That car's my pride and joy.'

'I've seen you polishing it.'

'You don't need me to tell you that kind of thing happens. But here, a fortnight ago, same thing again.'

'That's bad.'

'It's *atrocious*.' He lowered his voice. 'But I found out who did it, through a man who knows a man who knows a policeman. The family's notorious, they're telling me. Now, Harry, this is it. I'm not the kind of man to let a thing like that pass. But, and I'll admit it, I'd appreciate a wee bit of back-up. And, eh, I don't want to go in the Jaguar. Your car would maybe fit in better round that district. I mean, it wouldn't be recognised.'

He had been carrying two rectangular boxes in the carrier bag. When I looked over my shoulder as we drove through the scheme, I saw them lying side by side, where Walter had taken them out of the bag and laid them carefully on the back seat. I noted uneasily that the streets weren't entirely deserted. At this hour I had expected them to be, but we passed not one but three separate walkers, each hurrying on, head down, as if taking part in a foot race.

'Best to stop here,' Walter said. 'The house we want is round the corner.'

He got out and stood with his head back, searching perhaps to see if there might be a moon hidden behind the clouds. From the back seat he lifted out the two boxes, and I took one from him as I clambered out.

'Hope I can manage this,' Walter said. 'The bones at the bottom of my back are just a crumble, but I swim every day to keep the musculature. We're not allowed to dive from the side, so I dive from the steps. And just as I do, my body remembers what it is to be young. I look forward to that moment every day.'

We walked round the corner and Walter straightened his shoulders, cleared his throat and, reaching into the box, threw the first egg, chucking it overarm like a soldier lobbing a grenade. Another four followed in rapid succession, before I came awake and launched my first missile.

I didn't really believe any of it was happening until my egg exploded against the wall, leaving yet another dribbling mess on the white harling. There were a dozen eggs in each box and I was down to my last one when a light came on in an upstairs window. I started at a run after Walter, who had taken off like a startled rabbit.

In the car, as one street whirled into another, I crouched over the wheel and marvelled at the steady beating of my heart.

'Urban guerrillas!' Walter shouted, grinning and nodding. 'Just for one night!'

From then on, we alternated silence with sudden fits of triumphant guilty laughter. By the time we got back, the guilt had a slight edge and, wary of getting involved in a post-mortem, I refused his offer to come in for a whisky.

'Sleep well, then,' Walter said. 'I'll have one on my own, or maybe two.'

'Another time.'

'But you enjoyed it?'

'It was different.' I saw him smile at the word. Suddenly more light-hearted, I added, 'That's worth something when you get to our age!'

He pulled a card from an inside pocket, and passed it across. 'My son in Washington sent me that.'

It was a folded letter-card with a picture on the front. Angling it to catch the light from the streetlamp, I saw that it showed three old men. One was gesturing with two fists, one was stepping back in a trance of admiration, the one in the middle was leaning forward to join in whatever was going on. And there were two spectators, younger men, not part of the group but watching humorously. The caption read: ' "Growing old: it's not nice, but it's interesting." August Strindberg (1849–1912).'

'Unusual name,' I said, handing it back. 'I used to know someone called August.'

Home again, I shovelled the tablets into the glass of whisky, put the whole concoction into the pan of the small downstairs lavatory, and flushed it away. I looked at myself in the round mirror above the basin and wondered what Eileen would have said if she'd been watching. I offered her an explanation: Since the heart attack I'm warned off spirits; and imagined her smiling at the joke.

In defiance of doctors, back in my own familiar chair I cradled a fresh glass of whisky. As I sipped, I felt my heart beating. If it had been the last night turning into day of my life, it would have been one free of pain and full of interest. That might not be everything but it was a great deal; and in the end perhaps something a creature of chance and time should settle for.

I drained the whisky and went to bed but, habit being hard to break, got up and started my round of switching off lamps and checking the locks on every door and window. In the kitchen, the earliest flush of morning light drew me out to walk round the garden, feeling the dew strike up through my slippers. A small breeze was clearing the last traces of mist and the air felt newly washed.

The next thing I knew I was walking along a street, having just come from my house. Across the road I saw a man getting out of a car and opening the boot. I had started to walk on when he called to me and I saw it was my friend Tony. He was pushing a pram and he looked very well and smiling though he's young to have a family. 'I didn't realise it was you,' I said. 'I was expecting you further along.' As we turned back to the house, I was struck by how beautiful the child in the pram was. I can hardly talk to Tony for the wonder of her. Her eyes are incredibly blue and she is laughing. I can hardly wait to hold her in my arms. Tony asks about getting the pram in – we'll have to go up steps to the front door, I say, and since the kitchen is at the back we'll have to carry the pram through the front room. As I work this out, I become embarrassed and begin to apologise. I'm sorry, I'm sorry, I'm sorry. I can't stop, over and over again, I'm sorry, until I force myself to wake up.

When I opened my eyes on a milky darkness, I thought that something terrible had happened and then I saw Eileen sitting in her chair near the window with a blanket round her shoulders. Involuntarily, a breath of content sighed from me, but so softly she gave no sign of having heard. Almost at once, I decided against disturbing her. Lovers, even lovers for a lifetime, have need of times apart. She would be warm under the blanket, and when she was ready she would come back and lie beside me. It was enough to see her and know that I was complete. In the quiet night, I thought of how it was only by chance we had met and gone on to share so much together. It was a wonderful thing and a commonplace thing, an everyday miracle. I was a boat on a wide stream among so many others, on either side, ahead and behind, all of us drifting under the white moon and a mist rising from the water. After so long a day, I was ready now to sleep.

Good night, my love.